The three Barnhardt women are close—so close they're driving each other crazy . . .

Molly—at 18 her best friends are Elizabeth Barrett Browning and Emily Dickinson, as she dreams of the Mediterranean while she's stuck in Venice . . . Venice, California, that is

Shera—who's always been the belle of the ball, but lately with too many boys for her own good

Momma—who can't cross the street without consulting the Tarot cards

What's a sister to do?

The
Sister
Act

Blossom Elfman

*This low-priced Bantam Book
has been completely reset in a type face
designed for easy reading, and was printed
from new plates. It contains the complete
text of the original hard-cover edition.*
NOT ONE WORD HAS BEEN OMITTED.

RL 5, IL 6+

THE SISTER ACT

*A Bantam Book / published by arrangement with
Houghton Mifflin Company*

PRINTING HISTORY
Houghton Mifflin edition published November 1978
Bantam edition / October 1979

ISBN 0-553-12802-7

Published simultaneously in the United States and Canada

PRINTED IN THE UNITED STATES OF AMERICA

With love, for the brothers and the sisters:
Daniel, Richard,
Judith Faye, Marie

And thanks as usual to the Endore group: Emily Artz, John Davies, Henrietta Endore, Bob Lees, Betty McKenzie, Fran Yariv, and, of course, to Guy himself, who is still with us.

Chapter One

CLEOPATRA WAS FINISHED *and she knew it. Antony looked up at her with grieving eyes. "I am dying, Egypt, dying!" She turned to her handmaidens in despair. "Give me my robe," she said. "Put on my crown. I have immortal longings in me." She laid the deadly snake against her breast* . . . I would wait one more hour. The phone might still ring. If not, it was the asp for me.

All I did was glance toward the phone. Momma saw me. She stalked around me where I lay curled up with my complete Shakespeare trying to be anonymous. She lit a cigarette, which she swore on Bibles she would never do again. She bent to give me deep critical looks until I had to fan away the Pall Malls so I could breathe again. "Brilliant," she pronounced, "without an ounce of common sense." Then she turned on Shera who sat daydreaming as usual, not doing her homework. She pushed back Shera's hair to get a definitive look at her face. "And this one is gorgeous and she won't lift a finger to pass the tenth grade. God knows what will become of them." She phoned Mrs. Casamira to come over and read the cards.

It wasn't just the smoke in Momma's house. The air seemed thinner. My skin was getting too tight and I couldn't find a way out of it. I dreamed of sitting on a balcony over the canals of Venice, Italy, with soft Mediterranean sounds and the slushing of water, and I was stuck in Venice, California, in a tacky frame house with a sofa that still had the plastic cover on it, and Momma's dime-store prints of famous English hunting scenes, and her *ivy* which climbed out of pots and dishes and boxes, on tables and up over doorways, waving little green tendrils at me. I used to dream that the ivy was weaving itself over me. I was choking in ivy. I wanted to look back on all this with nostalgia and write little stories about it, but I was still *stuck* in it.

Mrs. Casamira opened the door tentatively to check the drift of things. She saw Momma's state. She set up the cards on the dining room table and lit one of her stinky Moroccan cigarettes. "Who am I reading for?" Momma gave us the "look."

"Read for Shera," I said. "I'm busy."

"I can see what you're busy with," said Momma, pulling us up to the table, Shera on one side, me on the other.

Mrs. Casamira took a drag at the cigarette and set it at the edge of the table. You could tell the history of prophecy at our house by the number of cigarette nicks. She took a deep breath to clear the tobacco out of her lungs and let in the cosmic forces of the universe. She turned her prophetic eyes on Shera. Shera let out a little nervous quinch. Her nicotine-stained fingers hovered dramatically over the card. She flipped it up to where Shera could see it. "King of Diamonds! She'll have great fame and fortune!"

"Didn't I tell you?" said Momma. "Great fame. Just make a little more effort. You'll make me so proud. You'll pass tenth grade and then if some contest comes along, well we'll see."

"I am trying!" said Shera in distress. "Tell her how hard I'm trying, Molly!"

"She's trying hard," I said. "Please leave her alone."

Mrs. Casamira turned her prophetic eyes on me. She breathed in inspiration and turned a card. "Knave of clubs," she said ominously. "Danger in foreign travel and fortune through education."

"Mrs. Casamira darling," I said, "the Oracle of Delphi is only supposed to give hints and clues. I'm not starting college in September, so forget it."

"She'll drive me out of my mind," said Momma.

"Turn up another card for me," said Shera anxiously, "and see if I have great love."

Momma let out a dramatic moan. "Great love! I'm talking survival in a world full of disasters and she's asking about great love. What am I going to do, a woman alone with two foolish daughters? Do you know how hard it is these days to find substantial husbands? What will become of them? I want the two of you to swear . . ."

"Momma," I said, "we're getting too old for this."

"Swear! If you go through college and get your teaching credential, you take care of your sister. And if she makes us all proud and passes high school and finds great fame and fortune, she takes care of you."

"Blood oath," said Shera. "I'll get the pin."

"I'm not taking any more blood oaths and I'm not getting any teaching credential," I said, "so cut it out."

"*I* swear," said Shera. "I'll never leave you out of my luck."

"What do you want me to do?" asked Momma. "Get hit by a car some afternoon coming home from work and float through eternity worrying about you?"

"All right!" I said. "Don't float through eternity. I swear."

"God is listening," said Mrs. Casamira.

"I *know* he's listening. I swear!"

"All I'm saying," said Momma, "is that if anything happens to me, I want to know that the two of you are watching out for each other."

"Stop smoking," I said. "You'll probably live forever."

"I *will* make you proud," said Shera. "I *am* trying."

"Gems," said Momma, kissing us both, "if they'd only stop worrying me to death."

"Gems in a world of thieves," warned Mrs. Casamira.

"And Molly will show me a little common sense and get a teaching credential," said Momma. "Wait and see."

"A teaching credential is life insurance," said Mrs. Casamira. "Ask my niece in Minneapolis."

"I know!" I said. "I *know* about your niece the teacher in Minneapolis." *Let all this be nostalgia soon. Let me write little stories about it, like* I Remember Momma. *Help me my handmaidens!*

I waited until eight. I said all the magical numbers. I said little prayers out of my childhood. I made vows to Momma's God and to Zeus and to Loki, the trickster, who seemed to be guiding my life. I began to turn to stone, like Socrates, from the feet up. The phone rang at nine.

"I love you," I said into the phone.

"One of these days," said Jason, "you're going to say that to the wrong person and get yourself into a lot of trouble."

"Who else would I say it to? You're the one I love."

"Look," he said, "this isn't going to work. You're a sweet . . ."

"Don't *say* that to me," I said. "If you call me a sweet kid, I'll throw up."

"You are a sweet kid, but it won't work out. So take it easy, Molly, and take care."

"It will work out," I said. "I'm sorry about the other

night. I thought you understood. If I had any idea you'd get so upset and *macho* . . . and I do love you."

"I don't want to hurt your feelings," he said, "but love isn't Elizabeth Barrett Browning lying on a sofa wrapped in a rug reading sonnets. I'll see you in a couple of years."

"We *can* make it. I'm perfect for you. Let's talk about it at least."

"Don't you ever take no for an answer?" I held my breath. I heard him hesitate. He who hesitates is lost. "Okay," he said. "I'm running over to the Getty Museum in the morning. I'll pick you up. Please be ready. I'm not up to facing your mother at eight in the morning."

"Momma only got suspicious because you wouldn't look her in the eye. She's not so bad when you get to know her."

"What am I doing?" he asked. "I'm out of my mind."

"It's because you love me," I said, "and you won't admit it yet. The heart selects her own society and shuts the door. I think your heart is shut on me."

"Who said that?" he asked.

"I got it from Emily Dickinson."

"Emily Dick . . ." A click. Disconnect.

That was all right. He was my Hamlet, my melancholy Dane. I was the one who could coax a smile out of him. And I was sort of weird, I admit that. I wasn't everybody's cup of tea. But I was his. It *had* to work out.

The Mona Lisa looked in my direction and gave me her Gioconda smile.

"He *did* call you," said Shera, making a place for me where she curled with her pillows and her dolls and all the leftover hard candies of her life. She loved to suck on sweet things. "I knew he'd call you again. So what am *I* going to do then? You can't go off to Europe or someplace and leave me alone with Momma. I'll die!"

"Then don't hang around the house so much. Join a few clubs or something. Get into drama maybe."

"I hate that school," she said. "All the teachers have it in for me. 'So you're Molly's sister.' You know how they do."

"I'm sorry. I can't help it if I went through first."

"And I can't make grades like you and they look at me funny."

"It was just as bad for me when I was fifteen," I said. "So get yourself something to pass through it."

"What?" she asked bleakly. "You have your books and all." She reached behind the bed for her old dog-eared copy of *Little Women* and sifted through her candy box for a sour cherry ball. "Read to me."

"You're getting too old to be read to," I said. "Start reading to yourself."

She lay back tugging at a coil of her hair. She had thick loops of hair like burnished gold and eyes as green as clear lake water. "Do you think I could get to be Miss Teen America or something? Then I could fly around the country making commercials and I wouldn't have to go back to that dumb school." She looked vague and uncertain. "I just hate when Momma isn't proud of me, and what substantial man will want me if I don't pass high school?"

"Who wants a substantial man, Shera? That's just Momma's junk. Do you want to marry an insurance man from Des Moines, Iowa?"

"I don't even know where Des Moines, Iowa, *is*. I just don't want to end up like Momma, scabbing around with nothing. What if something does happen to Momma? What will become of us?"

"Nothing is going to happen to Momma, so stop worrying."

"I can't help it," she said. "I'm so scared half the time."

I hunted for a sour lemon to suck. "I know. So am I.

Momma really meant well but she made us weird. We have to work ourselves out of it. So pull yourself together. You'll make it."

She hugged her calico doll and sucked her candy. "It's so easy for you," she said.

I waited on the front porch dying until I heard the asthmatic motor of his ancient classic Fiat. Then I ran back to the kitchen to try to become nonchalant. He came around to the back door. "Let's go," he called.

"Come in and have some coffee," I said. "You look half asleep."

He stood there undecided for a moment, framed in the doorway, resting his weight on one leg the way he did sometimes when he was thinking. His hands on the doorjamb were so marvelous, like the hands of Michelangelo's *David*. And his eyes on me, so palely blue, so tender, yet so cynical and wise. Then he walked past me and took a cup and poured himself coffee and straddled a chair and sat, trying to wake himself up. I loved the way he did that, he had such a flair. Like a ballet. I wished he would go back and do it again, so I could feast on it. He sort of looked through me until the haze of his eyes cleared. Finally he focused on me. "I should have my head examined," he said, "fooling around with little Mary Sunshine."

"You are my morning and my evening star," I said, "prince of the apple towns, famous among the barns."

He studied me for a while. "Who said that, 'prince of the apple towns'?"

"Dylan Thomas."

"Don't you ever have anything to say for yourself?"

"I haven't lived yet," I said. "I haven't got anything yet to say."

He raised his pale but tremendously expressive eyebrows at me and pursed his mouth, sort of pensively, and then that little tender look came into his eyes and he leaned over to kiss my cheek. Cleopatra and Desdemona and Ophelia and Juliet, they all sighed.

"I wanted to," I said. "The other night, I mean."

He covered his eyes with his hand. "Please forget it. Don't embarrass me."

"I want to do everything," I said, "and try everything in the world. But it's just that I can't until I leave Momma's house. I made her a holy vow. She's so medieval and old-fashioned. I just freeze up. It will be different once I get away. I just want to honor her while I'm still here."

He sipped at the edge of his coffee and said nothing.

"It's only two weeks. I swore to her I'd graduate with honors and make her proud, then I'm leaving. It's understood."

"Leaving for where?" he asked.

"Whither thou goest. Greece. Italy. Someplace with warm water. I'll lie on the rocks like a lizard and swim in secret coves."

"You can't swim," he said.

"You'll teach me. You'll teach me everything."

He smiled. A small almost held-back smile, but enough for my heart. He leaned over to kiss me, on the mouth this time. Momma walked into the kitchen. Bad timing. He straightened up, very uncomfortable. "Good morning," he said to Momma.

"Jason's here," I said.

Momma lit up a cigarette and narrowed her eyes on Jason. "I can see he's here. Does he know you have to go to school?"

"I'm cutting my first class," I said. "It's okay. My papers are all in."

"You have a perfect record," she said. "You're cutting nothing."

"All the seniors cut before graduation," I said. "And we're going to a museum. It's educational."

Momma fixed stone eyes on him. "What do you do for a living that you can go to museums at eight in the morning?"

I saw his face darken and his brows furrow. This was *not* what I wanted. He got up and started for the

door. "I'll see you tonight," he said. Not a word to
Momma. I thought she would stab him with her eyes.
Then he was gone. The rasp of his motor, and nothing.

"How could you do an awful thing like that!" I said
to Momma. "I only asked him here so that you could
get to know him better! Why did you chase him off?"

"Good riddance to bad rubbish," she said.

"What do you *mean* bad rubbish! He's a brilliant
mathematician! He's a friend of Eileen Cotter's brother!"

"What's a brilliant mathematician doing in a torn tee
shirt going to museums at eight o'clock in the morning? Why isn't a brilliant mathematician making substantial money in a computer plant or somewhere?"

"Because he's dropped out for a year to explore the
aesthetic side of his nature!"

"In English, please. We don't all have your brilliant
mind."

"He wants to be an artist."

"Artist," she said. "That's what I thought. I suppose
he wants to paint you naked."

"*Momma,* he's not that kind of artist. He dribbles
paint on canvas. He's been trapped by form and he
wants to experience total freedom."

"Total freedom." She cupped the cigarette in her
hand as if I couldn't see it. "Forget this boy, Molly.
He's not for you."

"You can't tell me who to like anymore," I said.
"I'm almost eighteen. And you promised me you
weren't going to smoke."

She tapped the head off the cigarette, dropped it in
a drawer and closed it. "Are you telling me I'm not entitled to give some guidance to a foolish girl who loses
her head over a boy and lets him come into the house
and put his hands on her? You think I didn't see it?
And he looks me in the eye and gloats that he's having
his way with you?"

"He wasn't gloating and I'm not saying you shouldn't
tell me how you feel! I love and respect you. But

please try to understand that my world isn't your world, Momma. My world is wide. It's not substance, it's essence. It's Athens, Greece, with lights on the water."

"What will I do with this girl?" said Momma. "She lives in clouds. What is there in Greece? Mrs. Casamira's niece spent a week in Greece. It's fried fish and waiters and smells and dysentery. If you need lights on the water, go to the Santa Monica Palisades. People come in tour buses to see the Palisades. Now go to school before you're late. You'll graduate with a spotless record and make me proud."

"I'm *going* to school and I'm *keeping* my record spotless, but right after graduation I'm leaving. That's understood."

"By you," she said, "not by me."

"What do you mean not by you! *It's understood!*"

"Stop screaming," she said. "And tell the truth. I said if you graduated with honors, I'd think about it. Well I thought about it and I see a young impressionable girl I wouldn't even let go to San Francisco let alone the sinpots of Europe with the murderers and the rapists and the white slavists."

"*Mom*ma, there are no white slavists in Paris, France!"

"The time isn't right," she said. "And you're still needed here. Have you looked at your sister lately, how pale she is? I think she's coming down with mono again. She's going through hard times. What sort of sister are you that you'd run out on her when she needs you the most? We're a family. And until the time is right, you can start school right here in L.A. This is one of the best schools in the country."

"I know! They come here in tour buses to go to that school! When will the time be right? When I'm thirty-five?"

"Don't be smart, Molly. I said we'd see how you develop next year."

"But it's my money! I saved it! You have no right to keep me here!"

Her eyes were beginning to tear. "Eighteen years of taking care of you and suddenly I'm not your mother anymore?"

"You know I didn't mean it that way! But I have to leave now! My heart needs to be free!"

"*My* heart needs to be free," said Momma. "But did I ever run off and leave you and your sister? I had plenty of chances. No. The time is not right. And believe me, one of these days when you're walking down the aisle with a substantial boy, you'll thank me for keeping you from doing a foolish thing."

"*I am leaving in June so please adjust yourself to it!*"

"And run out on your sister when she needs you the most?"

"*I don't need to stay here in L.A. just to baby-sit my sister!*"

Shera walked into the kitchen, pale and distressed. "Stop yelling at Molly. Nobody is asking her to baby-sit me. I don't need a big sister to baby-sit me."

"I didn't *mean* it that way!" I said to Shera. "Only she's driving me crazy!"

"*Go* if you want to," she said. "I don't need anybody hanging around just to take care of me." She started to cry and ran out of the room.

"Now look what you've done," said Momma. "Are you satisfied? I blame this boy. Before he came along, we were a happy family."

"*Who* was happy? *I'm* not happy and *Shera's* not happy, so *who's happy?*"

Tears welled in her eyes. "You mean I'm a bad mother."

I felt like Judas but I couldn't stop myself. "You hang on to us, you don't let Shera make friends on her own, you pamper the life out of her . . ."

"*Stop talking about me!*" screamed Shera from the other room.

"Go then if you feel that way," said Momma. "I can't stop you." Her hands were shaking and her eyes were wet.

"Jesus Mary, am I going to be stuck here forever?"

Mrs. Casamira popped her head through the kitchen doorway to get the lay of the land. She looked at Momma and at me, and pushed through the doorway carrying a plate of cake and a pot of coffee. She pulled me down to the table and poured me coffee and shoved cake in front of me. "Let her go to Our Lady of Sorrows. They have a new young priest. He knows how to handle girls when the blood is hot."

"I am not going to any priest!"

"My niece in Des Moines," said Mrs. Casamira. "Same thing. Worse even. Hot blood. Now she's married to a substantial dentist in Chicago and she drives a Mercedes."

"Mrs. Casamira *sweetie,* how come you have only two sisters and a *thousand nieces?*"

"Disrespect," said Momma. "When in her life did she ever show disrespect? Is this how you treat people who love you?"

"But she has a niece for all seasons!"

"I'm not insulted," said Mrs. Casamira. "It's the cusp of Aries. Let her take long walks."

I slammed out of the house. Like Alice, I fell and kept falling, past doors that were too small for me to get out.

I slumped through French. I messed up Victor Hugo. After class Monsieur Shulberger came and stood over me clucking his tongue. Monsieur Shulberger, with his polyester cravats and his rotten accent. *"Qu'est-ce qu'il ce passe avec* our Molly?"

"It's raining in my heart the way it's raining in the town," I said.

"Your Verlaine sadness? What's the trouble, my little cabbage?"

"I have a right to get away, don't I, Monsieur Shulberger? Isn't that right? *Ceuillez votre jeunesse?* Gather your rosebuds while you may? You read it to us a thousand times."

"Pauvre petite," he said. "If I advised all my French Six girls to go out and gather rosebuds, their mommas would put my head in the guillotine."

"But it's the law of nature, isn't it? For birds to leave the nest? It's my right, isn't it?"

He tugged at his cravat. "Talk to Mr. Wilkensen in English Lit. He has tenure. And work on your Hugo. I don't want you to go to the university and disgrace me."

Et tu, Monsieur Shulberger? *Merci beaucoup!*

I ate lunch alone, struggling with the problem. I consulted my friends. Lady Macbeth came and told me to screw my courage to the sticking place. Then I saw she had blood on her hands. I ran along the wild fields, an *inebriate of dew,* with Emily Dickinson. Then she went back to her lonely room. I ran out on the African veldt with Ernest Hemingway, so he had to put a gun in his mouth and blow his head off. Everywhere ambiguity. Then Jason beckoned to me. He took my hand and helped me to climb the jagged rocks and led me to the golden ship that lay waiting in the harbor. He sat me in the golden chair and waved to his friends to weigh anchor. Wind hit the sails. We dipped into the water, leaving the siren voices behind us.

Across the quad I saw my sister sitting with some basketball player, looking up at him and laughing and tossing back her hair. All her crying and whining that she didn't have any friends at school. Well there were enough boys around her, weren't there? She didn't need me.

Nobody was talking to anybody. Shera looked hurt when she saw me and Momma was highly offended. So I waited on the front porch for Jason to pick me up. He hit the horn for me. I saw Momma scowling through the curtains. Let her. We drove out to the beach and climbed onto the little rock jetty, those tarry rocks that always took me far from home, at least when the tide was high and waves hit them. I half closed my eyes, trying to see Agamemnon at the prow of his ship, face to the wind and the name of Clytaemnestra on his lips. Good luck. Only some drummers on the beachfront getting ready for a wild Venice night, one guitar, not too good, and somebody's transistor radio.

The air was cold and Jason sat with his arm around me sort of playing with my hair. "I hate to be the one to get you so down."

"It's not you, it's Momma. She wants me to stay here another year. My heart feels like an apricot pit." He leaned against me—heart, sinew, veins. I could sense the pumping of his blood. "I am leaving though. They'll just have to get used to it."

"If you were leaving," he said, "you wouldn't be sitting here agonizing over it. You'd just split."

"I am splitting. I just hate the thought of the two of them muddling around being miserable, that's all."

He stroked my hair. "Poor Molly."

"Please don't *poor Molly* me!" I kicked off my shoes and climbed down off the rocks and ran along the surf. I stood at the ocean's edge and let the fringes of water wash my feet, the same fringes that touched Japan and the islands of my dreams. I am nobody's *poor Molly.* I heard Jason call me but I ran along the shore. I sat on the sand and made myself a little burrow.

Jason squatted beside me and scraped the sand from my legs. He pulled me up and walked me back to the rocks. He put an arm around me and kissed me, but only on the *fore*head.

"Go ahead," I said, "dump on me. That's why you asked me out tonight, isn't it?"

"Don't make me the villain," he said. "I told you I was leaving in June."

"I am too!" I said. "I'm leaving in June." But he didn't pick up on it. "I *am* leaving, right after graduation. I'll go with you."

He held me against the damp. And then he let me go. "Come on, I'll buy you an ice cream."

No, you cannot comfort me with apples. The roof of thy mouth is wine, and the fields are hot and the scent of mandrakes is on me. "I'll work it out. She'll understand. If she doesn't, she'll have to get used to it. I'm drying out down here. I'll shrivel up and turn to leather. I will go. Just wait until graduation."

He said nothing. But his fingers against my cheek were so warm. I wanted to feel them warm forever. "We'll go out tomorrow night," he said finally, "someplace special."

I didn't like the sound of it.

He drove me home. I stood by the side of the car until he drove off, and I stood at the curb for a long while watching after him.

The whole house was going crazy getting Shera ready for a date. She got to go out with all those knuckleheads, and nobody screamed at *her*.

"Why are you so angry with your sister?" asked Momma. "It's just a school dance. She's been looking so peaked, maybe it will put a little color in her cheeks."

"Are you ready?" called Shera from the kitchen. "I'm coming out now!"

Out walked my sister, in a long green velvet skirt and a beaded blouse and a Spanish shawl that I swear was the same one Mrs. Casamira used to dress up her dining room table for séances.

"Do you like it?" Shera asked me.

"You look like an organ grinder's monkey. What have they got you dressed up for, *Gone with the Wind?*"

"What's the matter with it?" she asked, distressed. "I think it looks beautiful."

"Why are you still letting them dress you up? Why don't you dress yourself for a change?"

"What are you mad at *me* for?" asked Shera. "What did I *do*?"

Well she hadn't done anything, had she. It wasn't her fault that I felt raw and miserable. "I'm just being rotten," I said. "You look beautiful." I hugged her and tried to make it up to her. "I hope you have a super time."

"You too," she whispered. "I want for both of us to have luck."

The doorbell rang. I could smell him through the door before I opened it. He must have taken a shower in Brut. He was seven feet tall, his neck was long and red, and he had a gardenia in a box. Shera stood posed in the doorway, with the bright shawl and the green velvet. Mrs. Casamira had stuck a rose in her hair like a flamenco dancer.

"You'll have my daughter in at a decent hour," said Momma. Shera said something about being late and whisked him out of the house.

I went to dress, but my heart wasn't in it. When I came out, Momma and Mrs. Casamira were still fussing. "Did you talk to your sister?" asked Momma. "About you-know-what?"

"You wrote it with ink on her petticoat," I said. "If she doesn't understand about you-know-what after your five million lectures, she's deaf."

"Why are you in this terrible mood?" asked Momma. "You're going out with that boy again, aren't you. After what I said."

It wasn't fair. "Why aren't you telling me to go out and have a good time and come back with roses in my cheeks like you tell Shera? Why does she go off to a good time and I get warnings?"

"Because Shera is still a child playing," said Momma, "and you're a woman playing, and women get burnt."

Something was rotten in Denmark. A restaurant with cloth napkins and a whole bottle of French wine, and crêpes with ratatouille. I didn't like the smell of it.

He poured about a half-inch of wine into the bottom of my glass and shoved my plate toward me. "Why aren't you eating? You're always talking about going to the south of France to eat ratatouille. So here's ratatouille."

I couldn't swallow. "You're filling me up with crêpes to let me down easy. You're going to shove me off a cliff filled with crêpes."

His neck flushed and then his face. He poured himself a glass of wine. His mouth was so tense. I didn't want that. I reached over to touch his face but he took my hand away. "Why are you making this hard for me?" he said. "I told you my life was at a crossroads."

"I understand that! My life is at a crossroads too! It's our destiny!"

He leaned across the table. He looked around the room to see we weren't being overheard. "I cannot," he said in a lowered voice, "I can*not* get mixed up in all this crap you're in. I'm taking one year to make some sense out of my life. One nice quiet uncomplicated year."

"You can *have* an uncomplicated year! We'll rent a little shack somewhere in Greece, on an island. You can work on your art or your numbers and I can write. I'll cook fish for you and at night we'll drink retsina and talk."

"Retsina? How can you drink retsina when you can't even drink domestic wine without getting dizzy?"

"I'll learn to drink wine! You'll teach me!"

He downed a whole glass. I never saw him do that. His fingers on the glass were so tight I thought he'd break it. "You know what you are?" he said. "A hermit crab. You're crawling around looking for a shell and dammit, Molly, I am not that shell!"

Wham across the head with a pig's bladder. "Who's a crab? Since when am I a crab?"

He leaned across the table intently, flushed in the

face. "Not a crab, then, a snail. You know what snail. You read me the poem yourself. *The lark's on the wing; the snail's on the thorn . . .*"

"Pippa? You mean *Pippa Passes?* How am I Pippa?"

"Because you skip around in your little poetry world and you don't even see the thorns. Well I happen to understand you, Molly, but a lot of people won't. And when I think of you like that little innocent walking the mean streets singing that God's in his heaven and all's right with the world without seeing the crap around you . . ."

"You mean Momma? There isn't any harm in Momma. She's just sort of blank about the world, that's all. And she only has me and Shera, her little chaste daughters, and she loves us. I just have to wean her away from me."

"It's not just your mother! It's this fantasy you live in. If you want to be chaste, then dammit *be* chaste. But not because your momma wants you to. That momma happens to be choking the life out of you. And your sweet innocent sister sleeps all over town and you're the only one who doesn't seem to know it. And I'm not going to be around to pick up the pieces when it all hits the fan. Do something! Wake up or get out."

A dark wave washed over me, like death. "Why did you say a thing like that about my sister? Why would you want to make up a thing like that?"

He looked around. I was talking too loud. "Don't get upset. I was only trying to do you a favor. I didn't think you'd get this upset."

"*Who* said it? You don't even know my sister!"

"I know Richard Cotter, Eileen Cotter's brother."

"Eileen Cotter? That bitch? You know what she did to me in grammar school when I was ten? She untied the strings of my bandana halter, in front of the whole boys' kickball team! Why are you listening to Eileen Cotter? She's just jealous of Shera!"

"Okay," he said. He reached over to take my hand but *I* pulled away. "I'm sorry. I thought I was doing you a favor. It's a lie, then. I never should have told you."

"Liar!" I yelled. "Dirty bastard liar!"

He tried to maneuver me out of the restaurant. I carromed between tables. I took a swing at him. "Dirty rotten sonofabitch liar!" He put a hand over my mouth. I bit it. He tried to drag me out, but two other women grabbed him and asked if I wanted the police. Someone hit him with a purse.

"Do I need this?" he said.

I ran. How do I know where? I just ran. I ran with my eyes closed half the time. I dropped once out of breath at a bus stop bench. Liar! He wasn't Hamlet, he was Iago. I ran until I couldn't any longer, and then I walked. Until it became anesthetic, and all I could feel was the night air and the blood pumping in me. Then I went home. Momma was sound sleep across her bed with all her clothes on. Waiting for us probably. I wanted to see Shera, but she hadn't come in yet. She was still dancing her heart out on the crowded polished gym floor, her gardenia corsage pressed limp between her and the basketball player, her eyes full of stars. How *could* Jason? Why?

I asked all my poets.

They stood around me staring and saying nothing.

I guess I slept. I awoke cold in the thin light of the one lamp. I heard something. I sat up. Shera was walking across the room carrying her shoes. "Shera?" I whispered.

I don't think she expected to see me. She let out a little squeal of alarm and ran to her room and closed the door. I went after her. She was sitting in the dark. I closed the door behind me and turned on the light. "What time is it?"

She looked chilled to the bone. "Does Momma

know I'm still out?" she whispered. "Was she waiting up for me?"

"Momma's asleep. Where have you been so long? The dance must have been over hours ago!"

She sat shivering at the edge of the bed, hugging herself. I could feel the cold crunch of sand under my feet. And her skirt was wet and crushed. She was *sea*-damp! Her hair smelled of iodine and the sea! She crouched on her bed, half in shock. "He said he wanted to go to the beach. He said he wanted to run in the surf."

"At this time of night?"

"He wanted to. He wanted to go swimming!" Her teeth were chattering, not with cold.

"In *what* did you go swimming?" I could see sand all over her arms and in her hair. "What else did you *do* but swim?" She fell to the bed and pulled the covers over her head. I pulled them off. "What else did you do?"

She reached for her calico doll and pressed it to her face. "He made me. He made me do it."

"What do you mean *made* you? Did he force you?"

"You don't under*stand*! *Please* don't tell Momma," she begged. "I'll die if Momma finds out. I'll die if anyone finds out. Please don't tell anyone in the world if you love me!" She collapsed on the bed and cried with her head under the pillow.

Hamlet leaned against the arras, watching me. *I don't lie. I know a hawk from a handsaw when the wind is north by northwest.*

I pulled the pillow away. "What else have you been doing? Who else forced you? Momma's been giving you lectures about good-night kisses and you've been sleeping around!"

"Don't look at me like that!" she pleaded. "You don't understand."

"No I don't," I said. "I don't understand anything anymore."

"Please don't talk like that. Don't *you* talk like that, not to *me!"* She cried like a kitten in little mewing sounds with her head under the blanket.

I walked back to the center of the house, to the heart of it. I was sick. *Sea*sick, with disappointment and anger and longing. I couldn't even swim because Momma had told me I would drown and I believed her. Like I couldn't drink wine, like a million things I couldn't do. And there was Shera, crying her eyes out that she was afraid of school and this and that, and I had to stay home because of her, and *she* had run along the beach at midnight with her lover and *she* had lain on the damp sand looking up at the stars and *she* had swum the wild waves.

I went to my room and pulled my old suitcase out of the back of the closet. I began to throw clothes into it. Well, I was getting out!

Where was I getting out? A wave of heat, like panic, rushed over me. I couldn't get my money out of the bank until morning. And where was I leaving *for* without Jason to take me? Athens. I would go to Athens and stand over the pit of the Oracle and let the intoxicating fumes drive me wild with excitement. Was there a charter plane to Athens? Then I remembered that I couldn't even fly to San Francisco without getting claustrophobic with fear that the motor would conk out. I'd sign on a freighter, then, and hop off at Corfu and live in a shack by the water and eat feta cheese. Only I suffered from mal-de-mer. I puked all over the deck going to Catalina with the Girl Scouts.

So that was the truth, wasn't it. Jason was right. It was all fantasy with me. Jason had told the truth. I lay down on my bed to think about it. I felt heavy and dead. My eyes were lead. My heart was a rock. *Being* was too difficult. *Nothingness* was preferable. I wanted to sleep. So did Desdemona. We were both terribly sleepy. She took my hand. *Put out the light,* she said, *and then put out the light.*

"Where are all the happy faces in this house?" called Momma. "I'm making buttermilk pancakes!"

I lay dormant on the bottom of the sea. As long as I lay with my face in the cool sand, I didn't have to rise to the surface. So I rested in the soft silt, swishing my fins. I heard Shera's little tapping at the door. She came into my room. I felt her weight at the side of my bed. I tried to swim away but she pulled off the covers. She bent close to me. "I have to talk to you," she whispered.

"No you don't," I said.

"Please don't *be* like that. I can't stand it when you're mad."

"I'm not mad," I said. "You just do what you want to do and please let me do what I want to do. Okay?"

"Why are you talking to me this way?" she asked in alarm. "You just don't understand."

Momma came into the room. "Fine daughters. Nobody woke me to tell me the news. You let me sleep like that all night. And here you are sharing sister secrets and nobody invites me."

"I have homework," said Shera. She ran to do homework.

"You see?" said Momma. "Now she's happy and she's ready to work and make me proud. Are you getting up?"

"I'm sick," I said. "Let me sleep."

"Sick with what?" she asked.

"Just leave me alone," I said.

"Something is the matter. Is it that boy? Did he do something to you?"

"I only wish he had," I said. I crawled down into the blankets and waited for passage to my watery cave.

Once I awoke in darkness and saw Shera standing at the side of my bed. "You hate me now," she said, half in a whisper. "At least I had *you*. Now who do I have?"

I joined a small school of mackerel and swam for the dense seaweed.

Once I awoke in a hot sweat, breathing heavily.

Once I got up and tried to bite my knuckles hard enough to make myself cry. Then I thought how dumb that was, and I stopped.

Once I awoke saying, I don't believe this.

I opened my eyes to find Momma and Mrs. Casamira standing by the side of my bed.

"Look at her eyes," said Mrs. Casamira. "She's possessed."

"The only thing she's possessed by is that bum artist," said Momma. "Maybe this will shake some sense into her head."

The next day was a blurred day. I was weak from staying in bed so long. In my head somebody said, *Do something*. Well I was going to do something, any minute now. I tried to picture myself house-hunting in Greece. But I didn't speak Greek. I could manage some French. So I would start in France. I tried to get out of my bed, but my legs had turned to lead. *Move!* I lay back. Tears blurred my eyes. It was just dreams and cobwebs. Virginia Woolf beckoned to me from the sand and slowly I drew my robe around me and walked toward her. She took my hand and the two of us stepped into the sea and walked slowly toward the sun, until the waves washed over us.

From that faraway place I even imagined that I heard Jason's voice. "Just let me see her for a minute!"

Did I hear him say that? I pushed toward the surface.

"She's sick in bed," said Momma. "She can't have visitors."

"I'm here!" I called. "In the dark tower!"

He must have fought his way down the hall. He opened my bedroom door. "Put on a robe!" called Momma over his shoulder. Jason closed her out.

He looked ragged. He hadn't shaved or anything. He was highly upset. "Why didn't you answer when I phoned? Are you being vindictive or what?"

"I wasn't told," I said. "I was sort of submerged."

He pulled up a chair and collapsed in it, as if the wind had been knocked out of him. "What's the matter with me? You wouldn't even know how to be vindictive." His soft under-watery blue eyes fastened on me. "You look like a drowned cat."

"Very close to truth," I said.

"I must have been out of my head to think I was doing you a favor. But all I could think of was leaving town and you stuck here. How did I come to say a thing like that about your sister? What do I care what she does. How could I be such an insensitive bastard, with the mess you're in?"

"Also very close to truth."

"Oh you poor kid," he said.

All right, I will settle for pity.

He opened his arms to me. That's what you do with drowned cats. You hold them and warm them. Apollo opened his bright cloak and took me in. I put my arms around Jason's waist and spoke into his ribs. "I'm sorry I bit your hand. The way I felt, I'll probably give you rabies."

"I never meant to hurt you." He kissed the top of my head and my cheek. "We've always had such a good time together."

"You were right about me all the way around," I said. "I'm scared of everything. I was coasting on your coattails. I never meant to do that. But I am getting out. If I have to die of seasickness on a banana boat."

"Don't you think I understand?" he said, stroking my hair. "Don't you think I'd help you if I could?"

"Hey," I said, "I know that. I'll send you a postcard from the Foreign Legion."

He leaned back, looking worried. His eyes rested on me, then inward, he cracked his knuckles, he argued

with himself, he breathed deeply through his nostrils
and then out between his teeth. Then he leaned toward
me again. "Look . . ." he said.

Everybody looked. Desdemona, Virginia Woolf,
Pippa, even Quasimodo, from his bent position, looked.

" . . . I'm leaving in a few weeks for Mendocino
. . ."

"Since when? I thought you were leaving for
Greece."

"Who said Greece? *You* said Greece. I only said I
wanted to work near the water. You never listen to
what anybody says. I told you I was going up to Mendocino to try to work things out for myself. Either I
have something to say with paint on canvas or I don't.
And if I don't, I'll have to swallow hard and forget it.
Do you know what that means? Teaching math for the
next thousand years. So I'm taking this nice uncomplicated summer, a working summer. Do you understand me?"

We all leaned forward to understand him.

"So you won't get to Greece right away. Start small-
er. Mendocino is a rocky coast like the Aegean. I'll
drive you up. I'll help you find a room and a job.
You'll get a taste of being on your own Then I work
and you work. If there's time, and if we both feel like
it, we can walk a little and talk a little. Do you get the
drift of it?"

"I get the whole message," I said. "You don't love
me. I'm a real basket case. You're sludged down with
guilt and compassion, so you're giving me a ride but
you won't have time to baby-sit me. And if I survive
the voyage, we can have an *espresso* and walk along
the beach."

"Don't put it like that," he said. "I just want you to
know that if you think you're hooking into something
substantial, you're not."

"Jesus Mary, who wants substantial? You know
what happens to substantial? It dies on you or runs out

on you or gets taken away from you. I only want essence, and that's you. I happen to love you, in my fashion, believe it or not."

He put his wonderful long-fingered hand on my cheek. "I know that," he said.

Of course he never protested his own love. But as Cleopatra said to me, *It's better than being mummified.* She cast off her robe and her crown, and stretched her golden arms to the sun.

I could see Jason having second thoughts. He tousled my hair, the way you do with a puppy dog. "Your mother will probably shoot me."

"As soon as I get on my feet," I said, "I'll book a passage to India and get out of your way."

"I didn't mean it that way," he said. "I only meant . . ."

Well he wasn't sure what he meant. And Momma was rattling the doorknob. "Take it easy," he said. He fled. I never saw anybody actually *flee* before. You had to see Momma's face to understand it.

Momma inspected me for damages. "Are you all right?"

"I am now," I said.

"Why," she asked, *"why* do you need this? Why do you want to rush into trouble with open arms? A brilliant girl like you with all your chances."

"Please leave me alone," I said. "You don't know anything about it."

"I don't know?" she said. "I don't see a foolish girl who runs after a boy and throws herself at him?"

"I know what I'm doing," I said.

"She knows what she's doing," said Momma. "Two days on the brink of death because a boy said something to hurt her feelings, and she knows what she's doing. How am I going to survive with these two? This one sick over a boy who isn't worth the ground she walks on and that one coming down with mono."

It wasn't mono. It was me. I had been so rotten to her. Was it her fault I couldn't swim? She was as stuck as I was. So why did I have to turn on her like that?

I found her sitting in front of her dressing table, staring at herself in the mirror. She didn't even turn around when I came into her room. She spoke into the mirror. "You hate me now, don't you."

"I don't hate you, I never hated you, and I never will hate you. How could you think a thing like that? I just don't understand about you. I don't even understand about me, but I'd never hate you. How many sisters have I got?"

"You're leaving after graduation," she said. "I heard you through the wall."

"Sort of leaving," I said.

"It's leaving anyhow," she said. "You're breaking up the three of us. You're leaving me here with Momma."

"What else can I *do?*" I said. "I want to help you but I have to help myself first, don't I? When I figure it out, I'll be back. I'm not just deserting you."

She ran a finger down her cheek. "Go then," she said. "What do I care."

"I care," I said. "I want to talk about it now."

She shrugged her shoulders. "What for? You'll be gone. So forget it." Tears came into her eyes. "I still love you."

"*She*ra . . ."

She went to bed and pulled the covers up over her head.

"I don't like the way either of you look," said Momma. "So I took some money out of the bank and I put a deposit on a little cabin in Arrowhead. For two weeks, right after graduation. It costs an arm and a leg, but it will be worth it to see a little life in the two of you for a change."

"I won't be here," I said.

"Don't start up with me," she said. "I waited for years to see a Barnhardt daughter graduating with honors up on the stage. Don't start this argument again and spoil it for me."

"It's just a dumb graduation," I said. "And I only want to be on my own for the summer, just to get my head together. I didn't say I wouldn't go to college. I just said I'm not ready yet."

"You're almost a woman," said Momma. "These are hard times, Molly. You have to put away these childish ideas."

"Look," I said, "Friday I graduate. I'll walk onto that stage and make a Barnhardt speech that will go down in the annals of school history. I'll make you so proud the glow of it will last for a year. And when we get home, we talk. I mean a serious talk. Agreed?"

She hugged me and kissed me. "Don't you think I understand how hard these times are for you? These are the rapids. Once you're through them, it will be smooth sailing. Just trust me."

I packed my suitcase and set it at the back of my closet. I cleaned out all the drawers of my life. I shredded up all my old childish dairies. I packed away all my books. Good-bye Nancy Drew and your little hidden staircases. Good-bye Heidi, how I loved your grandpa. I paused to harpoon a whale with a tattooed native prince. Hard work. I said a tearful good-bye to Emily Brontë. Heathcliff and I are off to the moors now. *I never saw a Moor,* said Emily Dickinson. *I never saw the Sea.* Well we'll see them now! Elizabeth Barrett waved her little lace hanky at me. Good-bye, we're off to the coast of Portugal!

Loki stamped his foot and laughed. *All you're getting is a free ride up the coast.*

Don't talk to me, I said. The journey of a thousand miles begins with a single step.

Arachne, the spider, began to weave.

"I want you to eat a good breakfast," said Momma. "This is the most important day of your life, next to your college graduation. On that day maybe I can breathe easy for once."

"I can't eat," I said. "I'm melting. It's hot as Egypt."

"And see if Shera's up. I'm worried to death about her, she looks so pale."

Shera was sitting in front of her mirror, the way she had been for days now, like a sad Narcissus. "Please don't be like this," I said. "I'm expecting you at the graduation. I can't make my speech without you."

"Why don't you stop it," she said. "You're making Momma proud. She'll be there. You won't need me."

"Please don't let's hurt each other. I do need you there. Why don't you talk to me anymore? Why can't I just go away for a while without everybody making such a production out of it?"

But she just stared at her image in the mirror. "I'm too dumb to make anybody proud. I'm going to be stuck here, just like Momma."

"Who tells you to *be* stuck here? Go do something to get out then. Go be Miss America! But not because Momma wants you to. Because you want it."

"You're just saying that because you want to leave," she said. "You don't mean it."

"I'll write you long letters," I said. "Maybe you can come up to Mendocino for a weekend or something."

"You have Jason," she said. "I have nobody."

"How can you have nobody? The boys hang around you like moths."

"You don't understand and you don't want to understand," she said. "I'll come and see you graduate though. I still love you."

What I expected from Jason was an express messenger with a single red rose and a note. *My heart is with you.* What I got was a phone call.

"So good luck," he said. "How is it going with you?"

"Terrific. Really super. Momma said she wished me luck on my journey and packed me a sack lunch. My sister will wave me good-bye from the dock."

"That bad?"

"It will be better when I'm gone."

"You sure you still want to go?" he said.

"You sure you still want to take me?"

There were pauses on both sides. "I'll pick you up in the morning," he said finally.

"On the corner. This time don't come to the house."

It was all so childish and stupid. I wore jeans under my robe. I adjusted my hat at a rakish angle, but I would never hear the end of it from Momma. So I straightened it. Everybody came in to say adieu. Good-bye Jan, good-bye Robert, good-bye Ellen. We didn't even know each other that well, and now we were falling all over each other with wet eyes. "Good-bye," said that pismire Eileen Cotter, leaning over to touch cheeks with me. "And good luck."

"Nemo me impune lacessit, Eileen," I said.

"You're such a brain," she simpered in her saccharine voice. "What is that, Latin for good luck?"

"The Count said it in *The Cask of Amontillado.* It means nobody insults me and gets away with it. So go brick yourself up in an alcove, Eileen."

"What does she have against me?" asked Eileen Cotter. "She's crazy."

Sans doute.

Speeches rippled around me like water down a stream. I watched Momma and Shera, where they sat with Mrs. Casamira in the first row. Shera, like a chrysanthemum, fluffy and lovely, pulling little strings out of her handkerchief. Be happy, Shera. Momma in a new summer dress, like an overblown chrysanthemum, with her hair teased too high, fanning herself with a program. Mrs. Casamira, the Oracle of Venice, in her usual summer black. I wanted to remember them exactly that way, like an old tintype picture in a silver frame. When they called my name, I knew it was the passage of something. I rose to speak with a sense of my destiny.

They met me in the lobby of milling graduates. Momma dabbed proudly at her eyes. "Did you hear how they clapped? Next to your wedding day this will be the happiest memory of my life."

"Cut it out," I said.

She gave me her seed pearls for a present.

"But I don't want these! They're almost your only jewels!"

"A gem for a gem," she said. "And when this one graduates and makes me proud," said Momma, kissing Shera, "she gets my black pearl ring."

"Leave me alone!" cried Shera. She ran out of the auditorium.

"It's mono," said Momma. "I knew it."

"It comes with the hot weather," said Mrs. Casamira. "Give her more salt."

My suitcase sat in the middle of the room like a time bomb. "I don't believe it!" said Momma. "With that boy? You're running off with that boy after everything I said to you?"

"That's not the way it is! He's just giving me a ride up north! I'm not exactly going *with* him, not in the way you mean!"

"Don't lie to me! I wasn't born yesterday!"

"I just need to get away for a while! He's helping me get my head together!"

"I can imagine how he's helping you! It's just an innocent summer vacation. Then take Shera. She needs a summer vacation too!"

"Stop yelling!" cried Shera from her bedroom. "Will you stop it, *please!*"

"Listen to me," pleaded Momma. "He's tricked you.

He's sucked you in. Why do you think an older boy like that is fooling around with an inexperienced girl like you?"

"He's not Methuselah! He's only twenty-three. And I'm almost eighteen!"

"It's not just the years. In some ways you're younger than Shera. He could have all the experienced girls he wants. But he likes your sweet innocence. And when you're not so innocent? When you're sucked dry?"

"Don't make him sound like Dracula! It's not the way you say it is! Please try to understand, Momma! I love him!"

"Love? You've been living too long in poetry books. Love is the honey he baits the hook with. Then you snap at it and he hooks you. He'll finish with you up north, and he'll leave you. You saw how you were after one little fight with him? How will you be when he dumps you and you're all alone up there without us?"

"It's not that way, Momma! Love exists!"

"The way it existed for me," she said. "I loved your father. He was sweet and honey, just like this boy. Then you came along."

"I don't want to hear this," I said.

"You have to hear this. He said love also. Then he took one look at the flower blown up and he ran. That was love. So I struggled all alone with you. Then I met Shera's father. All promises. He loved me. I loved him. That was real love. And then Shera came along, and the bills came along and the problems came along. Save me from love. Go love in haste and repent in leisure. You're not leaving with this boy."

"You always mix me up," I said. "But you're not mixing me up this time. Maybe I wasn't meant to be in Athens yet. But I need to be by myself. I'm not deserting you and I'm not deserting Shera. I'll come back in September, and we'll talk about it. If Shera needs me, she can phone me up there. Maybe I will go to school, but for now I need space."

"If you go," said Momma darkly, "don't come back."

The headsman lifted his ax. "You don't mean that."

"As God is my witness, if you leave us now when your sister needs us most, don't ever come back because we won't be your family."

I think I was trembling or something. I don't know how long because time sort of froze. I came out of that awful space filled with anger. I wanted to say something terrible. But I heard the shattering of glass.

It jolted Momma and me. "What was that?" asked Momma.

I was still disoriented. "I think it came from Shera's room. *Shera?*" I called. "What happened?"

She didn't answer.

"God in heaven," said Momma.

"Shera?" I ran down the hall to her room. *"Shera!"* I called again. Momma pushed behind me. I opened Shera's door. *Jesus Mary pray for us sinners* . . . I held Momma back. "Don't come in. Please don't come in. She's had a little accident." I had to force Momma away from the door. "She's cut herself."

Momma shrieked, like a banshee. "It's a judgment on me for what I said to my child!" She collapsed like a bag of laundry against the wall and slid to the floor. Oh dear *God.* I ran to the living room window and opened it. "Mrs. Casamira! Come *quick!"*

I ran back to my sister. She had hit the mirror with her hands. Shards of glass lay all over the table and on her lap and all over the floor. Her hands were cut in a couple of places, but they were deep cuts. "Don't move," I said. She sat simpering and staring at the cut hands. Blood dripped on her legs and on the table. I heard Mrs. Casamira's cry and Momma's moaning. "Call an ambulance!" I yelled out. I cleared away a place on the floor and walked Shera over to the bed. Blood dripped from her hands, all over everything. "Molly . . ." she said helplessly.

"I'm here," I said. I wrapped her hands in towels

and hugged her and rocked her. She leaned against me sobbing.

I was still holding her when the ambulance came. The attendant took her away from me. I went out to where Momma lay half-conscious on the sofa. I had blood all over me. Mrs. Casamira bent over Momma, praying with beads. "She's going to be okay," I said. "It was just an accident. She has only cut her hands. It's not that deep. She's all right."

"No accident," said Momma. "I told my child not to come back. God struck down my other child."

The attendant carried Shera out. They had bandaged her hands, but the blood seeped through. Mrs. Casamira tried to shield Momma's eyes but she saw. "Please don't come," I begged Momma. "Stay here. I'll phone you from the hospital. She'll be all right, I swear."

"God forgive me," said Momma, and she turned away.

The ambulance rolled through the terrible night, the turning lights splashing red on cars, on streets. The whine of the siren was Momma's cry. I tried to comfort Shera, holding her, stroking her hair. She whimpered, looking at her hands.

"It's going to be okay," I said. "I promise."

She looked up at me with sad and vacant eyes. "I'm sorry," she said.

"It was just an accident. What have you got to be sorry about?"

"Please don't hate me," she said.

"I don't hate you. Why should I ever hate you?"

"I wanted Momma to be proud of me," she said. "I wanted to enter a contest, but I was failing all my tests."

"*Please* don't talk about that now."

"So I cheated. I got them to do all my papers for me."

The ambulance was going too fast, and the motion

was making me sick. "I don't understand. Got who?"

"The boys. I tried to tell you but you wouldn't listen. I got them to help me, in exchange."

I listened to her blankly. "In exchange for what?"

"You *know*." She turned her face away.

Then I didn't want to understand her. "In *exchange?*"

"What else could I do? Nobody knows how dumb I am. They all say, she's so beautiful, and they don't believe I'm dumb."

"Are you talking about the schoolwork? Who cared about the damn schoolwork! Momma was just pushing you to make you study a little!"

"She wasn't being proud of me. And she was being so proud of you. So I thought, if I passed everything, she might enter me in Miss Teen America and maybe I'd win and I'd never have to go back to that school. I tried to tell you."

Somebody help me not to remember she tried to tell me.

"So what did I have then? Just my face. What good was that? I was sitting there looking at my face when I heard Momma tell you never to come back and all. Then I wouldn't have anyone. I couldn't stand my face anymore, so I hit it."

We rolled through the inky night in silence for a while. I wanted to scream or something, but the siren was already doing that.

"I don't want to spoil anything for you," she said. "Just stay with me until they fix my hands. Then I want you to leave with Jason. Let one of us be happy, at least."

I sat on the hard bench at St. John's, waiting to talk with the doctor. Around me snakes hissed from dark pits and coiled around rocks, watching me. Dante stood in the prow of his little boat, ready to descend. *Paradise lost,* he said.

But it all cleared when Jason came running down the

corridor. He stopped short, the breath out of him. I forgot I was still bloody. "It's hers, not mine. My sister's."

"My God," he said, sort of shocked. He sat next to me but he couldn't take his eyes off the blood.

"She got herself into a mess and she didn't have anybody to talk to. I was too busy with myself. Mea culpa." I wanted to beat my breast with my fist, but it would look funny. I just shrugged my shoulders.

"Where are your things?" he asked. "Let's get you out of here."

"Hey," I said, "I can't do that. It's my sister."

He was furious. He almost shook me. "Don't be an ass, Molly. Take care of yourself. Run like hell."

"Well I guess I can't do that. Shera's in a mess and Momma's sort of foolish, but they love me. They'd never run from me if I were in trouble. I mean, who else in the world would stick by me in a mess?"

He started to answer. I held my breath and prayed for him to answer, but he swallowed it.

"So I guess I'll just have to stay around until she's out of it."

He sat bent over, looking at his hands. "I'm sorry," he said finally. "I'm really sorry."

"Hey, so am I," I said. "So have a good vacation and so long."

"Why don't you stop that?" he said. "This is a real mess. Don't be flip."

"Well I can't say I'm dying and I love you and I want you to wait around, can I."

All Walt Disney's little animals of the forest, small birds and little deer with big eyes, they all said, *Can he?*

He paused, looked at the palms of his hands, then closed them. "I guess you can't."

"Probably a relief to you," I said. "Lets you off the hook."

"That isn't true," he said. I waited for him to say more, but he didn't.

"So good-bye then," I said, "and good luck."

"Good-bye and good luck," he answered. He got up and walked away, rolling a little like a drunken sailor.

Don't do that! Don't leave me without telling me you'll write or something! Don't *leave* me!

He turned a corner and he was gone.

Little children playing ring-around-the-rosy looked up at me with sad eyes and sang, . . . *ashes, ashes, all fall down.* Emily Dickinson, dressed in somber brown, came and sat beside me. *Parting is all we know of heaven,* she said. *And all we need of hell.* She held my hand for a while. Then the doctor came out and said it wasn't terribly serious, just a few stitches. I phoned Momma to come now and I went back to my bench and waited. All my poets were gone. Everyone was gone. I sat in a plain bleak hollow hospital corridor. I was a small mushy gray snail. I crawled back into my hard implacable shell.

Chapter Two

❧

IT WAS A hot summer, but I walked head bent as if into a wind. For a while I died every time the phone rang and not for me. But how many times can you die before despair? *My life closed twice before its close,* said Emily Dickinson. With me too. My heart sped when the mailman came and slowed when he left. *Dear Molly, a terrible accident befell me and I am totally unable to write. Except for the kindness of these monks who tend the monastery . . .*

After a while I gave that up and took sanctuary at the university. I signed up for summer session with the rest of the leftover people. I hid in the unsorted book room of the research library, walking the lonely corridors of random titles. *Birds of the Antarctic. Death in Auckland. Maroc.* Hot and cold places. I, on the other hand, was lukewarm. I had turned sallow. My heart was sallow. My liver and kidneys were sallow. My islands of Langerhans were sallow.

38

"Was it my fault?" Momma asked me with apprehensive eyes. "I tried my best. I never left my children alone, they were always clean, they were always fed, I always loved them."

"Nobody's blaming you," I said. Well I couldn't just blame her, could I? She meant well. And she looked worse than Shera.

"Things have a way of working out, don't they, Molly? Look how you stuck by her through all this. You were my right arm. I never would have survived without you. You're my gem." She cried and fussed over me. "God will reward you."

We brought Shera home again. Momma made the sofa up into a bed so she could watch TV. We comforted her with the dolls and the pillows and the candy. We spoon-fed her while her hands healed. I read all the old favorite books but she didn't seem to be listening. "Don't worry anymore," I said. "It's going to be all right. Everything will be different now."

"How will it be different? You're here and I'm here, just like before." She lay back and stared at the ceiling. "So nothing is different."

It was different. There was the old house, the ivy crawling up over the doorways fatter and greener. Only now a solid wall of something closed us in. The house still hummed and the TV droned, and Momma, who had quit her little part-time sales job, cooked in the kitchen, stirred and boiled and baked, so that Shera could get back her strength. "She has to start eating something," said Momma, "if she's going back to school in September to make us proud. This time she's learned her lesson, hasn't she, Molly? This time she'll buckle down."

I could feel the walls, like E. A. Poe's torture room, closing in on me. "Momma, you've got to stop going-to-be-proud of her. Be proud of her now, the way she is."

Momma looked at me blankly and hurt. "When was I not proud of my daughters? I love her with all my heart. But truth is truth, Molly. She's not as brilliant as you. She's not a strong girl. We have to help her."

"That's just it," I said. "Don't help her so much. Just let her find her own dreams."

"Some find," said Momma sadly, "some don't."

So it wasn't any different. I drifted back to the book room, and when I couldn't stand the isolation any longer, I met a few other pallid people. A boy named Phillip who never took elevators, and a boy named David who memorized a verse of Cicero every day, and two nuns who were studying geology. My entire social life consisted of drinking herb tea and discussing alluvial plains. My life was shadows, and daydreams.

I walked into a bar on the back streets of Macao, and slipped into a chair at a wicker table. The fan whirred overhead. I saw Jason at the door, pale from his long illness. He limped over to the table. He sat beside me and signaled the waiter to bring another Pernod. *I never thought you'd come this long distance,* he said gratefully. *I'm here,* I said. *I love you.* His eyes begged for understanding. *Come,* he said, *it's hot. Let's swim naked in the cove.*

Well who was I kidding? I was Molly Barnhardt, the laughingstock of the Y. I paddled in three feet of water with the preschoolers, and at that I kept my feet on the bottom. Old angers stirred, old frustrations. I breathed against the force field of fear that surrounded me. I could almost feel my breath against it. Something had to be different. One small thing. And that would crack the wall. A hairline crack, and through that crack, they would send Jason back to me.

There was a tide in the affairs of men. I knew that. If you took the tide, you sailed on to success. But if you missed it, all the voyage was shallows. That was my life, shallows. I looked up to God, who was supposed to reward me in heaven. Is that what You want for me?

He leaned on the clouds, resting on his great arms.

His voice rumbled like thunder. *I breathed life into you, I expect you to live it.*

Then why did you make me so frightened of everything?

I am creation! He thundered. *I am the poem, I am the painting, I am the flower in the crannied nook! I bed the bulbs down for winter so they can bloom again in Spring! I move the tides!*

Help *me*, then!

His voice softened to the swish of a sparrow's wing. *I help her who helps herself.*

Well I was no snail! I was nobody's *poor Molly*. I went to the student store and bought a bathing suit. I mean courage. I walked down the long path toward the pool. I changed and took my baptism in the cold shower. I entered the pool area. I only floundered when I smelled chlorine, and I think I cringed at the sound of my footsteps hollow on the tiles. I was chilled, not from cold. I watched with ancient envies while swimmers of the real world cut effortlessly through the water. I had the feeling I was cowering. I may have trembled. Because the teacher came over and asked if she could help me.

"Can you teach an abject coward to swim?" I said.

Her name was Giselle. People named Giselle were small and tight and did yoga and modern dance and swam like dolphins. And they under*stood*. "Fear of water?" she asked.

"And most other things."

She circled me, touching my stiff muscles with competent fingers. "How much do you want to?"

"Life or death," I said. "Is that enough?"

"It's a matter of love, you know," she said. "You have to love the water and trust it."

I felt salt tears, like seawater, come to my eyes. I trusted love once, and I had got dumped.

"Jump in and let's see you float," she said.

"Hey," I said, "if I could float I'd be halfway to China by now."

"Then hang on to the side and blow bubbles."

I could do that at least. I clung like moss to the side of the pool. I breathed. I ducked and let the bubbles rise like pearls. Shadows of other swimmers passed in Picasso-esque distortion. The tiles were diamonds. I breathed and ducked and blew until I was lightheaded. Jason swam by. *I am still being tended by monks and as soon as my legs are strong enough I will walk down the mountain and phone.*

"Okay," said Giselle, "it's time to let go."

"Not yet," I said. "Tomorrow."

"Now," she said. "Yield yourself to the water. Abandon yourself to it. Lie on it, like a mattress."

I looked down. No mattress. I could see the bottom clearly. It would be like everything else in my life. I would fall and crack my skull on the tiles. Another bump, another lump. "I'll probably die," I said.

"I don't think you've got much choice," said Giselle. "I think you've come to the jumping-off place. It's probably too late for you to go back."

Where I floated, it was reeds and marshes, nothing substantial to hang on to. Before me was the abyss. I had no choice. I released my fingers. I just let go. Panic seized me. *Die,* chuckled Loki, the trickster. I think he must have made me mad or something. That's what you think! I said. I yielded myself up. I became flotsam on the surface of my life. The water came up under me, like a hand, and held me suspended in time. I lay there astonished. I wanted to tell Giselle and I got myself unbalanced and floundered. She caught me and helped me get my footing. "Good," she said. "Now we'll start with the first stroke."

"Tomorrow," I said. "I'm afraid I might not do it again. It might be a fluke."

"You'll do it," she said.

I swam with the Olympic team all the way home. I leaped from the high diving board and soared like a bird. I plummeted, my head cut the water, I shot down, skimmed the bottom like a porpoise and leaped up in victory. I couldn't wait to see how my world had been transformed. Even the house. I would see flags of joy flying. And Shera waving at me from the balcony. And we'd kiss and cry and say good-bye and fly apart to the ends of the world.

The air stiffened as I entered the living room, acrid with smoke. Shera sat trapped at the dining room table. Momma looked up guiltily and urged the sorceress on. Mrs. Casamira set her cigarette at the edge of the table and held the I Ching sticks over her head.

"What are you doing! You promised me no more fortune cookies!"

She breathed in the air of prophecy and dropped the sticks. She bent quickly to read them. "You wouldn't believe this hexagon," she pronounced. "I see a career. In medicine." She coughed a few times, waiting for celestial messages. "A dental technician," she pronounced finally.

Shera looked to me in misery. "She has a niece, a dental technician, in Palm Beach, Florida, who drives a BMW."

"Enough!" I said. "Will everybody please leave my sister alone!"

She was alone, really alone. She lay disconsolate on her bed, staring up at nothing. "Why are you still hanging around the house?" I said. "Your hands are better."

"What's the use," she said. "I haven't got my strength back. So what's the use."

"Who says you don't?"

"Momma."

"Well do you or don't you?"

"I don't know," she said. "I don't know what to do about anything."

"Well you're not going to figure it out around the house, are you? Things don't happen until you make them happen."

She suffered indecision. She thought. She looked at me. "What can I *do?*"

"What you want to do. What you need to do to make yourself happy."

She hugged her doll. She sucked on a hard candy. She tugged at a lock of her hair. "Will it be all right?"

"If you make it all right."

She jumped up, stuffed a bathing suit and a towel into a tote bag, kissed me, and ran for the back door.

Momma was frantic. "Where is she? Where did she go? Did you let her out of the house, Molly?"

"I think she went to the beach."

"In her condition?" said Mrs. Casamira. "God help us. She'll start to swim, she'll get weak and drown."

"Or maybe she'll get eaten by sharks," I said, "or maybe her bus will get hijacked by Cubans. Leave her alone, will you please?"

Momma almost died until three o'clock. Shera walked in sunburnt, clear-eyed, and marvelous. Momma ran to fill her a hot bath before she caught pneumonia. "I met someone wonderful," Shera whispered to me. "I like him so much. I think everything is going to be all right now."

Except for the pain in my heart. His name burned on my lips. His dear face. The tender eyes. He was up in Mendocino not knowing how I had changed. So he hadn't written. There must have been a reason. I might just drop him a postcard. Just a friendly card. *Hello there, old buddy! From your friend, the swimmer. Molly B.*

Where was my pride? Pride *went*eth before a fall. The hell with pride. I pulled the phone on the extension cord into a closet and closed the door. I used a flashlight to dial Richard Cotter's number. When I heard his voice, I broke out into a sweat. I ordered my voice to be casual. "Hi! This is a friend of Jason's. And I lost his address in Mendocino."

"He's not in Mendocino," said Richard Cotter. "He's here in L.A. Who is this?"

I replaced the phone. I knew it. *I knew it!* Zeus and Hera, Mercury with his winged slippers, Apollo! They controlled my fate! I had pleased them and they had brought him back. I was wild! I was mad! "I'm taking the car!" I said to Momma.

"Where?" she asked. "Drive carefully. Watch out for buses. Stay off the freeway. Wear your seat belt."

Watch out for low-flying pigeons. Stay out of the head wind. I drove like a madwoman toward Jason's place. I had only been there once before. But I knew where it was in my heart. Hadn't I been there a thousand times in fantasy? A million times?

The studio was the top of an old converted grocery warehouse, off an alley in the oldest, most run-down part of Venice. He took the place because it had good early light or something. It was Rive Gauche. It was Montmartre. I parked somewhere, I hoped it was near the curb. I ran to the old metal door that was his entrance. The golden doors to my destiny. "Jason!" I looked skyward. From the little dormer window I saw his face. *His* face! He looked down on me. "You're back!" I cried. He motioned for me to come up.

You went up by a sort of stairway ladder. I rose *into* the studio. As if I had been submerged, and now I had surfaced.

The studio was changed though. I think it was. It all looked so bleak and barren, just the plain rough walls and the old beams, a naked bulb, the lone bed on the floor and an old Salvation Army sofa. All the color was out of the place. Then I realized that all the paintings were gone. *His* stuff.

Jason waited for me to say something first. What should I say? He was there, physically there, close enough to touch. "You're back," I said. "I can't believe it. Have you been trying to reach me? When did you get into town?"

He turned to his little two-burner stove and set a kettle on it and lit it. He reached up to the shelf for a box of tea bags. "About four weeks ago."

A thick curtain of fog seemed to drop between me and the world. "Four weeks?" I looked for a place to sit down. Then I didn't want to sit down. "Four *weeks?*"

He set out two cups for us. "It didn't work out for me in Mendocino. I don't know what ever gave me the idea I could paint. So I came back. I'm going to register for the fall quarter and finish my coursework."

I was stunned. "Four *weeks* and you never once phoned?"

He poured water over a tea bag. "You were busy with your sister and I was down in the dumps. What good would it have done?"

It wasn't real! All the while I was dreaming, he was here! "Four weeks and not even a postcard to say, 'Having a wonderful time, glad you're not here, but did you survive?' "

"I knew you survived," he said. "I asked about you and I saw you a couple of times."

"You *saw* me? Where did you see me?"

"At the pool. I guess you learned to swim. Your hair was wet anyhow."

He poured the tea and carried the two cups over to where I stood. "There wasn't any use. I knew you were tied up with your family. I knew you couldn't let go. It isn't anything personal with you. You were the best thing that happened to me all year."

He offered me the cup. I almost knocked it out of his hand. Anyhow I sloshed water. "Swell," I said. "I'm a first-class court jester. Next time you're in a depression, just ring me up."

"What did you expect me to do?" he said, drying his hand on a towel. "Stay around and watch you break

your heart over your sister? You have to grow up,"
he said. "It's a tough world. You have to know how to
save yourself when the ship is going down."

"Thanks a lot for the good advice," I said. "So I
guess I made a really dumb mistake, didn't I. You
know me, silly Pippa. Just one damn thing after another."

"Sit down and shut up," he said.

"Sorry," I said, "but I have a lot of things to do. So
welcome home anyhow. And don't call me and I won't
call you, okay? Good-bye and good luck."

I almost killed myself getting down the stairs. "Molly
. . ." he called after me. "Come back!"

"Can't!" I called. "I have to run!"

He called after me from the dormer window. "Don't
run, dammit! Come back and talk about it!"

"Who runs!" I called back. *"Who* runs!"

Well I ran. To the Exxon station. I locked myself in
the toilet and threw up.

"What's *wrong?*" asked Shera.

"Nothing," I said.

"I know when it's not nothing," she said. She
brought me her candy box and offered me the best
choice.

I lived in the pool for the next few days, so I could cry
without being noticed. If the pool turned salty, that was
me. Big fool! Dumb fool! To go running there when he
didn't give a damn! I invited Loki to strike me dead if
I ever spoke to him again. I wore dark glasses on cam-
pus. Nobody was going to feel sorry for me. I was sitting in the cafeteria not reading a copy of *Heart of
Darkness* when he sat down across from me.

He was furious. "Why are you making me the villain? What else could I do? Do you know how I felt
up there trying to work and thinking how I left you
down here in all that mess? And what about me? Did
you ever once ask what was happening to my life? I

told you I was in shreds and patches! I ended up throwing every damn canvas into the sea!"

"Don't blame me for your fits of frustration," I said. "It no longer concerns me."

"Sure it doesn't concern you," he said. "It never concerned you. *You* love, *you* this, *you* that. What do you know about love, you're so wrapped up in yourself. What about me? I sat up there in a goddamned tunnel! Without any light at the end of it! I'm going to have to teach math for the next hundred years! Do you know what that feels like?"

"Oh, no," I said. "I'm just a little dreamer. I don't understand pain and passion."

He slumped in his chair. "I didn't mean that. It's just that you live in dreams, Molly. You don't see the world as it really is."

"And you do?" I said. "How can you see the world when you live in a tunnel? You said it yourself. A tunnel without light in it! The trouble with you," I said, "the *trouble* with you is that you don't do anything that isn't practical! And you don't fall in love, so how do *you* know what love is? You don't love your math, you don't love your art, you don't love people. You see me in a mess and it isn't practical to hang around so you duck out. That's not life, is it? Tunnels are for beavers or moles. And even *they* come up for air to build little nests for their mates or something! How can you paint when you don't yield yourself *up* to life and just let it carry you? But you wouldn't know about that."

I mean who had a better right to say it than a woman who had swum a fifth of a lap?

He stared at me angrily for a while and then he got up and left.

That was Monday.

Well I just happened to be having coffee at the same place on Tuesday and he put down his coffee cup and sat for about a half hour watching me. I wanted to walk away but there was something I needed to read.

That was my only reason. He put his foot on my foot.
I would have moved it, actually, except that I didn't
want to communicate with him.

On Wednesday he bumped into me as I walked toward the gym and he kept bumping into me until he
bumped me into a clump of trees and held onto me as
if he were drowning. "Do you think I like being alone?"
he said. He tried to kiss me but I turned my face.

On Thursday I didn't.

"Why," he said after he kissed me, "why should I
get myself mixed up with somebody who's still stuck to
an umbilical cord?"

"Who asked you to?" I said.

"Do I need Peter Pan flying through the treetops
looking for a boat to take her to Byzantium?"

"You bet you do," I said. "You live in a tunnel. Why
do you think I was so good for you?"

"I'm out of my mind," he said. "You'll come back
into my life and just when I get used to you, you'll run
on me."

"Who ran on *whom?*" I asked. "You'll walk out just
when I need you the most, and who needs that."

"You're crazy," he said. "Don't come back if you're
not serious, Molly. I mean it."

"So okay I won't," I said.

"Why me anyway?" he asked. "I'm a washout as an
artist. I'll bitch about the math every day of my life and
I have a rotten temper." This he said with melting eyes.

"You're probably a wonderful artist," I said, "although it's no longer my affair. Only your talent is
coated over with lava or something. And Richard Cotter said you were brilliant."

"It's only numbers," he said.

"Euclid alone has looked on beauty bare."

I thought he would hit me, or cry. "Do you always
magnify people you love?"

"Who said I loved you anymore? Anyhow I see the
truth, that's all. Like the Emperor's New Clothes. I see
what's underneath."

"Please don't give me any more crap," he said. "Please don't say anything you don't mean."

"Crap? *Who* took crap from *whom* exactly?"

"Did I ever commit myself? Did you ever hear me commit myself?"

"Meaning?" I said.

This is it, said Anna Karenina.

This is definitely it, said Juliet.

Oh yes, my heart, said Jane Eyre.

"Meaning you're ready to get committed then?"

"What about your mother?" he said. "And your sister?"

And the I Ching. And the ivy. All of that. But I had got so *full* suddenly, like a seed in winter warmed by the rush of spring, and the husk begins to crack.

"I'm late for class," he said. He left me and walked away. Then he came back. "I wanted a nice uncomplicated year. So what did I get? A kite-flyer with a holy vow." I watched him walk into the landscape. He turned to look at me, then he was gone.

No he wasn't gone. He was here.

So what about it then? I couldn't think of one logical reason why I still loved him. Except for his eyes. And the turn of his head. And his knees and ankles. And his wonderful hands. His right hand looked like the hand of Michelangelo's *David*. Did I mention that? And he had come back and I wasn't alone now, and I felt alive for the first time, and that was truth, wasn't it?

"Brian is coming for dinner," said Shera. "Please tell Momma not to say anything embarrassing. I want him to like us. Please make Momma shut up for once."

As it turned out Momma liked him. Who wouldn't? A shaggy St. Bernard, big and fleshy, with a shock of soft brown hair and the most open honest eyes. He shook Momma's hand in his big paw and ate her fried chicken as if it were haute cuisine. "So," Momma began as she passed him more mashed potatoes, "are you still in college?"

"I'm in electronics," he answered politely. "I'm going into television repair."

"Very sensible," said Momma, "the way they make televisions these days. Do you live at home?"

"He lives alone," said Shera with compassion. "In a lonely room and he eats at restaurants. His mother is dead."

That touched Momma's heart. An orphan. She shoved more chicken at him. "And do you have brothers and sisters?"

"Only one sister," Shera answered for him. "She's a bitch and he hates her. One of these days he'll have his own business."

"Which makes you how old?" asked Momma.

"Almost twenty-two."

"And Shera is not yet sixteen." Her message was in neon. Brian looked hungrily at Shera, he reached out a hand for her, but withdrew it, the way you would with a delicate bird. He didn't talk much, but he was kindly and soft, with a touch of old-fashioned chivalry. I never heard Shera laugh so much. Her eyes flashed. She looked happy for a change. And he couldn't take his eyes from her. After dinner they talked, head to head, for hours. Until Momma got tired of him and turned on the television as a hint for him to leave. So they went into Shera's room.

"That boy is a grown man," said Momma. "Go tell her to leave the door open."

"This is the first time in months I've seen her happy," I said. "Leave them alone. He's a real Walt Disney."

You want to know who was alive? I was alive. And Jason was alive. And since we were brand new, we had to see the whole world again. We ran around town like crazy. To every museum, looking at things we'd seen a thousand times. To the science museum, to see the machine that showed laws of chance and probability with little piles of steel balls. We found the one that

was us. Then we went to Disneyland and took all the
kiddie rides. Some melancholy Dane, hunched up in
Mr. Toad's wagon. And we went to parks and beaches.
Sometimes we'd lie on the sand, side by side, noses almost touching, not even talking to each other. And I'd
become embarrassed because he was watching me and
I'd cover my face with my hands. And he'd take my
hands away.

"Well I'm not exactly a great beauty."

"You are," he said. "A great beauty." He lay back
and made canvases of the sky. "I wish I were big
enough to match your fantasy."

"Just wait," I said. "You'll see."

And he'd tuck me under one arm and build the sand
up around me like a snug harbor.

Nicely in port, said Captain Ahab.

The sky is not falling here, said Chicken Little, safe
under the big hen's wing.

Dear Mr. Rochester . . . said Jane Eyre, sitting on a
footstool and looking up at his big craggy face.

Waves spilled. Then sun went down and the moon
came out. From down on the beach somebody's cigarette glowed. There was no wind. Time was very still.
I think this was infinity.

"What is he?" asked Momma. "A permanent boarder?
Hospitality is one thing, but this is ridiculous. He's
put on ten pounds with my cooking."

Shera came in from her good-byes, flushed and ra-
diant. "Isn't he nice and respectful? You do like him, I
mean really like him."

"I like him," said Momma, "but enough is enough."

"He's very substantial," said Shera. "One of these
days he'll have a business of his own."

"Moderately substantial," said Momma, "for all in-
tents and purposes. But school starts on Monday so tell
your friend no more school-night dates."

"But you like him. You said you liked him."

"What is there not to like?" asked Momma.

"I'm *so* glad," said Shera, "because we're getting married."

"Over my dead body!" screamed Momma. "Do you hear me, Shera? *Over my dead body!*"

Momma banged on Shera's bedroom door but we'd closed it and shoved the bed against it. Then I laid into her. "Are you completely out of your mind? When did you dream up a crazy scheme like this?"

Momma hit the door. "*Do you hear me, Shera?*"

"Why are you mad with me?" asked Shera. "I thought you liked Brian!"

"Of course I like Brian. I'm crazy about Brian. But you're not even sixteen yet!"

"But you told me! You told me to grow up and make decisions! Well I did! I thought you'd be happy about it!"

"I told you? *I?* When did I tell you to get married?"

"Well you said figure it out, so I figured it out! I'm never going back to that school! I'll die if I have to go back! I told you that!"

"Then we'll change schools! You have a whole life in front of you!"

"What life? It's a nothing life!"

"But we talked about it all summer! You said you'd finish high school and maybe go to New York and learn to model or be an airline hostess."

"Well I learned what an airline hostess is! She's a waitress. Thanks very much. You'll probably be a famous writer or something and I'll be a waitress. Why are you being so mean? You've got Jason back. Why shouldn't I have somebody too?"

"Who tells you not to have somebody? Have Brian, go out with Brian, but don't get married when you haven't even grown up yet!"

"How *can* I grow up when I do one little thing and you scream at me as if I'm a baby! I love Brian and he loves me!"

"What will you get married *on?* He's just an apprentice! He hardly makes anything!"

"He'll have a job next June! And he can move in with us until then. He loves the way Momma fusses over him. He calls her Mother Barnhardt. Please this one time try to understand. I do lousy at school. They'll end up putting me in dumbbell classes and clucking their tongues over me. How beautiful she is and she has no brains. And too many boys know me."

Oh what a mess. "Are you sure you know what you're doing?"

"He wants me so much," said Shera. "And I want him. Please help me! Make Momma understand."

Momma struck at the door with her fists. "Never while I'm alive will you do a foolish thing like this! A whole golden life in front of you! I'll lock you up if I have to!"

"At least wait a while," I said. "Think it over."

"There's nothing to think," she said. "I *love* him."

"That much?" I said.

"More than my life," she said passionately.

We moved the bed. We walked out holding hands.

"Never!" swore Momma. "I forbid it! To tie herself down to the kitchen at fifteen when she could have fame and fortune? Not while I'm alive. This is my last and final word and nothing you can say will change it. Do you hear me, Shera?"

"I'm pregnant," said Shera.

"Jesus Mary," I said.

"Oh Mother of God . . ." said Momma.

"Why is everybody being so awful?" cried Shera. "I only did it so Momma couldn't break us up the way she tried with you and Jason!"

When Momma was revived, she said, "Spoiled, all spoiled."

Shera wept for half an hour and then threw up and I tucked her in with her dolls and her pillows and I brushed her hair out to calm her. "Can we talk about it now?"

"What's to talk about? I thought you'd be happy for me. And I thought Momma would be happy that I found somebody so substantial. I don't understand why everybody is being so terrible."

"You just took us by surprise, that's all."

"But it's so perfect now," she said. "I'll have somebody and I won't have to go back to school and all."

"I understand that you love Brian. But the baby, Shera. That's something else. Can we talk about that?"

"I *have* it, so what's the use of talk?"

I brushed out the long silken strands of her hair. "Having it doesn't mean *having* it."

"Get rid of it, you mean? I'd never do that! It's my baby!"

"What on earth will you do with a baby? You're just a baby yourself. Momma still makes your bed for you."

"Well you told me to start doing things for myself! So I am. Brian never had a family. Now he'll have a little family of his own. That's what he calls it. A little family of his own."

"Shera, a baby isn't a calico doll!"

She held on to my hand. "You said we were weird sisters and we had to work our way out of it. You told me to figure it out for myself. Well I figured it out. This is what I want. Please help me to be happy."

I made Momma a cup of tea and took it to her room. She lay across her bed crying, a handkerchief pressed to her eyes. "You're not helping her," I said. "Don't make her feel worse. It's not the end of the world."

"Do you need a volcano to spill on you," she said, "to see the end of the world? She had such a golden life. Now she has nothing."

"She has Brian," I said. "I guess he loves her."

She sniffled and blew her nose. "Don't talk to me about love. I told you and I warned you. Nobody listened. Now I have to live the pain of it. My poor child."

"She's not a poor child. She's pregnant and she'll have to work it out with Brian."

"What is there to work out?" she said. "She made her bed. She has to lie in it."

"Why is everything no exit in this family? She can still 'do' something about it. You know what I mean."

"To me!" flamed Momma. "To *me* you're saying this!"

"Then if she wants to, she can have it and adopt it out, or she can get married and keep it. So just calm down and give her a chance to work on it."

"She'll have to get married," said Momma. "Before people find out. Then after the baby they can separate and we can say she made a terrible mistake. God help her to survive this."

"I don't believe what I just heard," I said. "You're going to let her have the baby because of the *neighbors?* And then you'd bust them up? You'll break her heart!"

"Don't give me schoolgirl philosophy. Go find out who this boy is."

"Not me," I said. "I told her how I feel and I told you how I feel. Now it's her life and I'm not messing in."

"Who told me to keep the bedroom door closed?" she said. "I lay this on your doorstep, Molly."

"What I want to know," I said, "is how *I* got responsible for my sister's pregnancy."

"Whenever something happens with your family," said Jason, "your face turns sour. Isn't it time you got yourself out of there?"

"Out of where?" I said.

"Where do you want to go?" he said.

"Where do you think I ought to go?"

"Don't play games," he said.

"Who's playing games?" I said.

"Only don't move into my life if you haven't thought

it out, Molly. Don't come into my life if you're just going to duck out when the going gets rough. Think it over carefully. Okay?"

I looked around his bleak little studio. I decorated it with my eyes. A paper lantern like a fish to cover the naked bulb. A Mexican rug on one wall. A little wooden rack for the imported wines we would buy at bargains. And with me there he would paint again. Love did that. I stood at the top of the stairway in my peasant blouse and beads, my hair frizzed, greeting the guests of our *salon*. The writers and the artists. Come on in! Pour yourself an absinthe! The *espresso* pot is on! "Did you hear what I said?" asked Jason. "Think it over carefully. And take a good clear look at me, Molly. The way I am."

"You are my northern Star," I said, "ever fixed in my firmament."

"And you're Haley's Comet," he said. "Don't come until you're sure."

"Come where?" I said. "Say it."

"You drive me crazy," he said.

"I am not," I said to Momma. "I am not do you hear me *not* going to stick my nose in her business again. She wants to get married. You told her she could get married. Now it's her business and Brian's business. Leave me out of it."

"Why didn't he present himself at my house if his intentions were honorable?" said Momma.

"Shera says he's afraid to show his face. So you know who's to blame for that," I said.

"Those quiet ones," said Mrs. Casamira. "Nice plain boys, butter wouldn't melt in their mouth, and then they turn up Jack the Ripper."

"Heaven preserve us," said Momma.

"Not me. This is Shera's personal life. She has to work it out."

"A fifteen-year-old pregnant girl is entitled to a personal life?" asked Momma.

"Then get a detective," I said. "I'm not Sherlock Holmes."

I should think not, said Watson. *Nothing like him.*

Shera moved around her room like a sleepwalker, picking up something and then forgetting what she was doing and pausing to dream or sigh.

"I guess I never saw you so happy," I said, "but I wish you'd wait until you know him better."

"I know him," she said, "with my whole heart."

"Did he go to school out here in L.A.?"

She shrugged. "I don't mean things like that."

"What did he do before he got apprenticed? What are his friends like? Do you like the same shows and things?"

"I've never been to Laguna," she said. "Do you think we could have a little honeymoon in Laguna?"

"What does Brian want?"

"I'm embarrassed to ask him," she said.

She drifted in space. And there were Momma and the sorcerer's apprentice hunched over the dining room table, laying out the tarot. Mrs Casamira chewed the end of her cigarette, laid it on the edge of the table, and help up a card for me to see. Hanged Man.

"Find out," said Momma.

I mean, what was I supposed to do? You can't get married and have a baby just to get out of English Two. But she did love him. And stuck in Momma's house it would be worse. And if Momma messed in, Shera would only get hurt. So there I was outside the television repair shop at the marina, watching Brian through the window. In a white jacket, courteous and kind, smiling and talking to people. Some Jack the Ripper. Then he saw me and waved nervously and spoke to his boss and came outside and asked me to have coffee with him.

"I'll just level with you," I told him when we got settled into a booth at the coffee shop. "Shera sort of bowled us over with the news. I know you're both crazy to get married and Momma is still sore, so I'm acting as a sort of liaison to pull it all together. Okay? And if I'm butting in, just tell me to butt out."

His upper lip was sweating. "I don't blame your mother for being sore. I don't know how it happened. I love your sister and I respect her. I got carried away, I guess. I figured we could wait a couple of years until I'm settled in a job, but then she told me about the baby, and there was nothing else for it."

Now something wasn't clear here.

"But you're crazy to have a baby though. I mean you're dying to have a little family of your own."

"Before I have a decent job? I think it's foolish. I wanted her to get rid of it, but she told me about her deep religious convictions. Well I couldn't make her do a thing like that."

Tell the jury, said Perry Mason, *when was the last time you set foot in a church?* Shera cried into a little lace hanky. *When I was christened.*

"Look," said Brian finally, "it will be a little rough at first, but I love her and she loves me. If she's willing to stick it out, so am I. I never dreamed I'd be lucky enough to get anyone as sweet and as beautiful as your sister."

"Did you see him?" said Momma. "Will the sister stand by him? What kind of family? Are they substantial?"

Shera was culling through her wardrobe, deciding what to discard and what to keep. "Do you think I could get married in white and all? Nobody knows yet."

I shut the bedroom door, closing Momma out.

"What's wrong?" Shera asked in alarm.

"I went to see Brian."

"Why?" she asked. "Why would you see Brian without me?"

"Because you were walking around in the clouds

and Momma's got her nose in the tarot, that's why. Shera, you told me Brian was dying for a little family of his own."

Her face went pale. "What have you done?"

"I didn't *do* anything. I just want you to think the whole thing out before you decide for certain to keep the baby, that's all. I know you love Brian and I know he loves you, but if it doesn't work out with a guy you can always break up. You can't break up with a baby, Shera!"

"You went snooping behind my back!" she cried. "What did you say to Brian about me! He loves me! He does love me! He wants to get married!"

"I never said he didn't! It's the baby I'm worried about. I don't want you to rush into anything. I'm only saying think about it!"

"I did think about it, and I figured it out, and everything is perfect so why are you messing in and spoiling it!"

Momma knocked and came in. "What's the matter with you, Molly," she said, "getting your sister upset in her condition. I told you to find out about Brian with tact, I didn't tell you to get her hysterical."

"*Momma* told you!" screamed Shera. "Momma told you to break us up and you went?"

"I never went to break you up!"

"You lied to me!" she screamed. "You went behind my back because Momma sent you! I'll never trust you again in all my life!"

"I only went to try to help you!" I said, "and I'm sorry now I ever did!"

"It's too late for sorry!" she screamed. "I'll never believe you again in my life!" She moaned and wrung her hands. "Now who do I have to trust?"

"Okay," I said. "It's your life, so do what you want. Only don't blame me for anything."

"Stop this," said Momma. "Have some compassion in her condition."

"What condition? She has no condition. She's pregnant, and she wants to be pregnant. So just leave me out of it now, okay?"

"You never wanted me to have anything of my own!" screamed Shera. "You always wanted to be the top sister!"

"I *said* I'm sorry!"

"That's why you make me feel dumb and all, with your big words and your Shakespeare, so *you* can make everyone proud! I'll hate you as long as I live."

"That's it," I said. I walked out.

I went to my room and I packed my suitcase. She was right. It was her life. And if this is how she wanted to get herself out of Momma's house, then it was her business. But this was my life. I closed my typewriter and took a warm coat and filled my purse with as much junk as I could handle.

I came back into the living room packed for travel. "What are you doing?" Momma asked. "Don't we have enough trouble on our hands without your temperament?"

"It's time for me to leave," I said. "Tell Shera I'm sorry and I love her and I'll phone her later."

Momma tried to argue but Shera started to throw up.

Where was I going? I lugged my stuff down the street to the bus stop. I was going to Westwood to find myself a room in a dorm or something. Then the bus came along and I was so upset I didn't realize I was headed in the wrong direction. And by the time I got off again there I was a couple of blocks from Jason's place, and I was really tired and I needed a cup of tea so I dragged my stuff about eight blocks to the studio and dumped everything outside his door. "Jason!"

I saw his face at the window. I heard him coming down the stairs. He opened the door and looked at me and looked at my suitcase and stuff. "You're sure," he said.

"I'm not sure about anything," I said.

"Then what are you doing here?"

"I had the general idea that you wanted me."

"Did you have a blowout with your family again?"

"Sort of," I said.

"So you decided to camp out here until it blows over and then when I disarrange my whole life and go crazy with the sound of your typewriter, you pull up and go home again."

"How do I know?" I said. "I was drawn by magnets. I thought you said you loved me."

"Dammit I do love you, but you said you'd think it out!"

"I could write with a feather pen," I said.

I think he was frustrated. I think he was also nervous. Who wasn't. He carried my stuff upstairs. "Go argue with a poet," he said.

He went back to some work he was doing. But he watched me making a place for myself in his closet and setting up a little desk for myself on the kitchen table. When I was settled in, I sat in the little dormer window looking out at the street. I loved that window. So he came and squeezed in with me. "I guess I would never have got you here any other way, would I?"

"I'm the best thing that could happen to you," I said. "This place is so bleak. Wait until I throw a few manuscript papers around. And I'll learn to cook fondue. And I'll read you my poems. And you have so much to teach me. You'll never be bored."

"Maybe you'll be disappointed," he said. "I'm not Robert Redford."

"Who needs Robert Redford," I said. "I love Jason Hallem. Let me name the ways."

Am I doing this right? I asked Anna Karenina.

"Where are you?" asked Momma frantically. "We've been calling all the hospitals."

"Why would I be in a hospital with my suitcase and my typewriter?"

"Run over or mugged," said Momma.

" . . . or worse," said an anonymous voice in the background.

"Aren't things bad enough without this?" asked Momma.

"Take my number for emergencies," I said. She took my number. "Where are you?" she asked suspiciously. There was a small silence. "Are you with *him?* Did you run after him again? You couldn't be such a fool, Molly. Come home this minute or put a knife in my heart."

"I'm not putting a knife in your heart," I said. "I'm just trying to live my own life, that's all."

"Like she's living her own life?" asked Momma. "Come home this minute or never speak to me again."

Since I wasn't speaking to her, I hung up. "So that's that," I said to Jason. For no good reason I cried for an hour. Beautiful. Red eyes and red nose. Some romance. "I'm a bust at this," I said. "I'm not very sophisticated. It's only that she never froze Shera out so why is she freezing me out?"

"Stop complaining," he said. "You don't know when you're lucky."

"Do you want to throw me back?" I asked him.

"Not likely. I haven't got a TV. You're better than most of the shows." He made me a cup of tea and spiked it with a little sweet wine. "A start is a start," he said. "Only it would have been easier to fall in love with an orphan."

Momma didn't phone me. Only Mrs. Casamira, just in passing, did. "Hello, Molly. I just happened to be thinking of you so I thought I'd call and see how you are."

"I'm fine," I said. "How are you? How are the nieces?"

"You know that you're living in sin," she said.

"And how's Momma?"

"How can she be with a knife in her heart?"

"It's her knife," I said. "Let her take it out."

"You wouldn't be so cruel," she said, "as to refuse to come to your own sister's wedding."

"Of course I'll come," I said. "I'll even bring Jason so Momma can make it up with him."

"Over my dead body," said some strange voice in the background.

If that was the way she wanted it.

It was only a little ceremony with a justice of the peace. Nobody was there but Momma and Mrs. Casamira. Momma wouldn't even turn around to greet me.

"Please, Molly," said Mrs. Casamira, "don't keep this knife in her heart."

"Tell her all she has to do is meet with Jason and she won't have a knife."

"Never," said Momma. "I have two fools for daughters."

It was a beautiful mood for a wedding.

Shera sat in the little bride's alcove, at the edge of her chair, trapped in a long dress with a flower petal-bodice and miles of netting. "What on earth have they got you dressed up for!"

"She said it was for the pictures. That when people saw them in years to come, they wouldn't know how I got married." She held her arms out to me. "I knew you wouldn't let me get married without coming; I never meant what I said. I could die for saying it."

"I never believed it," I said. "I'm not mad. And you do look so beautiful."

"He does love me, doesn't he, Molly? I mean not on account of the baby?"

"He really loves you. So please be happy now."

"You said we were weird sisters," she said, "and we'd have to work ourselves out of it. Well we both did."

I guess she was right. She wasn't even sixteen yet

and she was pregnant and she was getting married to a guy without a job and she'd be stuck in Momma's house until June.

I, on the other hand, had taken a lover.

Chapter Three

❦

I<small>T WAS</small> almost Eden.

"It only needed a mural on the blank wall. A jungle with thick, lush vegetation and all the animals and the birds of the forest, and a tiger peering out between the trees. Only put a smile on the face of the tiger."

"The lady wants a smiling tiger," said Jason. "The lady gets a smiling tiger." He sketched it out on the wall. He and I laid in the color. You couldn't believe it! So thick, so dense you could almost smell it. We had to paint some vines around the other walls until they met, like arms embracing.

Tiger, tiger, burning bright. All we needed were forests of the night. So we cut a skylight over the bed so that we could watch the progress of the stars. Only L.A. has a heavy cloud cover some of the nights, and the neon of the city was so bright it obscured the stars. It didn't stop us. We found a comet's tail and Sirius and

Venus rising and the hand of the Hunter and black holes and supernovas.

And when we got tired of space, we squeezed into the little window seat and looked down on the mortal world, which was a little VW garage below. The guys moonlighted and the neon glowed in the shop window. Sometimes when they came out for a beer, they waved up at us.

Time was crystalline and sharp.

Then suddenly over coffee or eggs or something in the morning, we'd suddenly remember we were strangers. I'd see Jason staring at me and I'd get embarrassed. Or we'd be dressing and we'd suddenly become self-conscious and we'd run off to class. Then I'd be sitting in Economics or someplace listening to the romance of Adam Smith and I'd remember a certain incline of his head or a tendon in his foot and I'd almost die before I got back there to see it. Or maybe I'd get there first and sit waiting until I heard his footsteps on the ladder and he'd stand there out of breath looking at me, and I'd know why.

Then he started to talk. Slowly at first, then frantically, as if he had to get it out before it frightened him too much. About his family back in some bizarre place in Kansas. His father, who was a carpenter-woodcarver, and his mother, who was some kind of American Gothic math teacher, how his mother scorned his father, and how his father withdrew finally, and how his mother took him away to live in this cold mathematical world until Jason ran away, only to find that his father had died. I wept and Jason wept and we hung on to each other while he suffered the loss of it again. And how he had come out to L.A. on his own and how he had been a loner until he met me.

Then he made a little space for me and listened while I let out all my fantasies, and all my fears, and all my daydreams, about the night-light and how I dreamed my father would come back, and how I loved love but was so afraid it would be snatched away, the way horrible things in the night used to threaten to steal me away. Jason kissed me and painted a sign for me and hung it over the entryway. *Beware, forces of evil! Do not enter here!*

It was so odd the way we spun ourselves out, thread by silken thread. "Are you happy?" he asked me as we sat under the jungle trees beneath the tiger's protective eyes.

"Byzantium," I said.

Then Shera phoned. "Where *are* you? Momma's dying, she's so hurt. And we all miss you."

"Don't miss me," I said. "Come and see me."

"There? To Jason's place?"

"It's my place too," I said.

"Please stay and meet my sister. Come home and let's make it up with Momma."

Jason got into his running pants. "I'll jog along the beach for an hour. I committed myself to you. I never committed myself to loving your sister. If I get near that brat, I'll smack her behind."

I heard Shera calling from the street. "Where *are* you?"

I hailed her from my wonderful world-viewing window. "Up here!"

"Up *there?*" She looked puzzled.

I had to come down to help the little mother up the ladder. "Hey, you look wonderful." She really did. Her eyes were clear and green and her hair had these marvelous highlights and her skin had a glow to it. "Motherhood agrees with you." I was really glad to see her.

"What *is* this place?" she asked in consternation.

"These studios are hard to find," I said, "especially with good light." I moved her around my room, showing her my world. "This is the jungle and this is the paper lantern that catches the first morning sun translucent through the fins, and this is the sky, where we space-travel."

She moved away from the tiger. "Do you have that thing *look*ing at you all the time? I'd die. Where's the bed?" The mattress was made up on the floor with our little pot of fresh flowers beside it. "Don't you have a headboard even?"

"It's neat this way," I said. "And here's my little window, where I look down from the clouds and dream and write poems."

She looked out of the window. "That's a VW gar*age* down there! It's so awful, Molly. Does he make you live here?"

"He doesn't make me. I love it."

"You *say* . . ." She poked dubiously around the two-burner camping stove and the shelves Jason had put up for our dishes and the coffee table he had ingeniously made from a packing crate. Only she snagged her nylons on it. "Not even regular furniture," she said, really appalled.

"So how is married life?" I asked her.

She stuffed herself with sandwiches. "I'm eating for two." She leaned toward me with happy eyes. "It's so super being married. I told you it would work out. Nobody believed me and all. He's so good to me, Molly. When I throw up in the morning, he practically dies, and he runs to bring me ice cream night and day, and he feeds me with a spoon. Today he brought me flowers. For no reason. He just brought them."

"What about Momma?"

"She squeezes him fresh orange juice and practically puts on his socks. You know Momma."

"So I'm the only one she's mad at."

"She's just hurt because you don't call her. And she's worried about you. So am I," she said. "Look at the way he makes you live and all. Does he still love you, do you think?"

"Sure he loves me or I wouldn't be here, would I."

"Did he come around and say he'd marry you?"

"Shera, the last thing in the world I want to do is get married."

She buttered herself another sandwich. "Did he ask you and you turned him down or what?"

"The subject never even came up."

She raised her eyebrows. "Does he bring you flowers or candy? Does he feed you with a spoon?"

"Jason isn't a flower and candy person, Shera."

She frowned sternly. "He took advantage and he ought to marry you. I'll come over when he's here and have a talk with him."

"Shera . . ."

"Why shouldn't I?" she asked, not so innocently. "You did. With Brian, I mean."

I was starting to get a headache.

"I don't really mean it." She leaned over and hugged me. "I wouldn't mess in. I guess I just like being the top sister for once."

I wasn't sure how to take it. "Since when were we in competition?"

She poured more cream into her coffee. "We always were. Didn't you know that?"

"Then you meant all those things you said when you blew up?"

"Maybe I did then," she said, "but I don't now. I'll always love you. You're my sister. Who else have I got?" She took a last pitying look around the studio. "Brian's brother-in-law lives in San Marino. He has money coming out of his ears. He already offered Brian a job if he wants it. I'll never leave you out of my luck, Molly."

I thanked her and helped her down the ladder. I had such a headache. I tried to remember what she had said. Did I ever purposely make her feel dumb? Could I have *done* that? The afternoon had turned grayish and drab. I could see how the studio might look tacky in that light. I searched my memory for all the things

I had ever said to Shera. I mean, Momma was bad enough. She didn't need me to make her feel crummy. I put on some water for tea, but I had run out of matches to light the stove. My head was awful. "Stop grinning at me," I said to the tiger.

I must have been asleep when Jason returned. I came dizzily awake. "What's the matter with you?" he said. "Did she give you a bad time?"

"It was okay. I've just got a headache."

"Since when do you get headaches?"

"It just started."

All I needed was a little sympathy. But he wasn't sympathetic. In fact he was really sore. "You asked for it. This always happens with your sister. The way you feel about her, isn't it time you called it quits?"

"How do I feel about her?" I said.

"How do I know. Sore, trapped, maybe you hate her but you won't admit it. Ask Freud."

"Since *when* do I hate her? How can you say a rotten thing like that?"

He blinked at me. "Since when can't I say what I think? Weren't those the ground rules?"

"But it isn't true. I don't hate my sister. Sometimes she blows up or I blow up and we say things, but I don't *hate* her!"

"In a pig's eye," he said. "Go stick your head in the sand. Be an ostrich. Have yourself a headache."

"Why are you yelling at me?" I asked. "I've got a rotten head. All I asked for was a little sympathy."

"Why should I give you sympathy if your head hurts because you hit it against a stone wall?"

"Well thanks loads!" I said with what I suspect was a great deal of sarcasm. "I only asked for sympathy. It wasn't as if I'd asked for flowers."

He looked as if I'd slapped him. He started to answer, but then he didn't.

"Talk to me," I begged him. "My head is splitting."

"I haven't got anything to say."

"Don't be like that, *please*. This is the first time I've asked you for sympathy. Please don't be awful." Then I remembered the hospital. "No. It's the second time. You weren't too good about that either."

He turned and walked out. He even slammed the outside door.

I was horrified. What had I said to him? Why? I ran to the window to catch him but he had run down the street and toward the beach. I was not myself. My head was stuffed with cotton. Why couldn't he just have said something nice and rubbed my back or held my hand? Who wanted flowers? I had a whole tiger wall full of flowers. *Jason, come back!*

Only he didn't. I must have fallen asleep or something. When I awoke the room was darkish and the paper fish rattled when the breeze hit it and the tiger leered and the jungle got murky and I heard a rustling in the undergrowth. I began to get frightened, the way I did when I was little and Momma had to leave me alone in the house and she warned me to lock up and not let the murderers in. Murderers always hung around outside and scratched against the window-panes or squeaked in mouse holes. I jumped a mile when the phone rang. I ran for it. "Mea culpa! Come home now!"

There was a terrible moment of silence. "You come home," said Momma. "All is forgiven."

I sat in the window praying for him to come, watching for him, listening for the sound of his feet on the stairs. Nothing. He knew I was miserable. He knew I was waiting. Okay, if that's what he wanted. I went home to have dinner with Momma.

"You think I wanted to keep this silence?" said Momma. "Don't you think it hurt me every day that I did? But you're stubborn as rock. And I thought it would make you come to your senses. As God is my witness I never deserted you. I drove by every day and watched you coming in and out."

"Okay," I said. "Don't make a thing of it. I was only three miles away. You could have looked out the window and seen me. And I'm here now."

"You're thinner," she said. "He doesn't feed you."

"I'm not in bondage," I said. "I feed myself. I weigh exactly the same as the day I left. Anyhow I do most of the cooking."

"I can imagine you do the cooking," she said, "and the cleaning. He has a free housekeeper and he brings her to live in a barn."

"Who said I lived in a barn? *Shera!* What did you *tell her!*"

"Leave Shera alone. She's in the bedroom with her husband, waiting until I have a chance to see you alone. She didn't have to tell me how you were living. I knew it in my heart."

"Momma," I said, "why can't you just accept that this is how I want to live my life? Maybe happy for me isn't the same as happy for you."

"Happy? Was that happy, the way you sounded when I phoned?"

"That was something else," I said.

"Was it?" said Momma. "If I thought you were thinking clearly, Molly. If I saw he loved you with all his heart, if he had run after you the way Brian did with Shera, if he tried to carry you off on a white horse, if he showered you with presents to make you happy. Tell the truth. It was always you running after him."

I didn't say anything. What could I say?

"I remember how you felt the last time when you hardly knew him and he dumped you. Now you've fallen in with your whole heart. What will happen to you when he dumps you next time? My heart is breaking to think of it."

"Don't let your heart break." I had such a terrible headache. I was getting sick to my stomach.

"Well the door of this house is open," she said. "God

forgive me for keeping my selfish silence when my child needed me. Come. Let me give you a decent dinner for a change."

Shera and Brian reappeared. Shera looked guiltily out from the shelter of Brian's arm. "I didn't mean to say anything. I just couldn't stand the way you were unhappy there in that awful place. Please come home with us, where we can take care of you."

Brian kissed me and called me Sis.

I tried to eat dinner but nothing was digesting. Momma cried when I left.

I returned to the upper floor of a converted grocery. Nobody was home. An empty room. And it was cold. They never heated that place right. I switched on the naked bulb which was covered with a paper lantern, but the glow was grayish and thin. Everything looked pukey. Well I had run after him, hadn't I. He never actually asked for me. Never. He only took me in, like a foundling. Then when I had my first crisis, he ran. Great. Marvelous. I curled up in the little window seat but it was damp outside and the windows were wet. Everything looked through a glass darkly. Those old stores and the mean streets. My head began to hurt. I don't mean hurt, I mean migraine. Loki got in there and stamped around in boots. Jagged lines of lightning. I lay down on the sofa and tried to sleep. But it was cold and my head hurt. Hey, where is everybody? What happened? Now I had it, now I didn't. Like a magic disappearing act. Only everybody was gone, even the audience. *Help me!*

Edna St. Vincent Millay came to sit beside me. I haven't seen you in a long time, I said.

You haven't needed me for a long time. She looked at me sadly. *Thus in the winter stands a lonely tree nor knows what birds have vanished one by one. I only know that summer sang in me a little while, that in me sings no more.*

The light switched on. Jason stood over me, in his jogging pants, without a sweater. He must have been running and he was sweaty and chilled. "Finally," he said. "Where have you been?"

"Where have *you* been while I've been dying here?"

"You kicked me out of the house. I was running."

"Who kicked you out? I asked you for a little sympathy and you ran out!"

"*Who* ran out? I came back and waited for two hours! Did you go home to your mother again? What's the matter with you? You look terrible."

"I've got a migraine. I'm sick."

"You bet you're sick. Since when do you get migraines?"

"Since now. It came."

"What do you mean it came?" he said. "You went home and got it!"

"Please don't yell at me when I'm dying."

"*You're* dying! I've been running all over hell worrying about you, so what do you think I am!"

"Well maybe you're sorry I'm here then. I never said I didn't have problems, did I."

"That's one big problem, Molly. I told you before you moved in. *Move* in, only don't step in with one foot temporarily. I asked you that!"

"Who stepped in? Didn't I leave home to come live with you?"

"Did you leave home? You're only spitting distance from your mother's house! You paint yourself a jungle and you think you're a thousand miles from her, and the minute there's a storm in the forest, you slink home!"

"Well how could I come with both feet if you never asked me? You took me in like an orphan in a storm. You never actually asked me."

"How am I supposed to *ask* you when you fly space like an astronaut still attached to the umbilical of the home ship!"

"But that's not true! I'm only still around here because you have to finish your coursework! We can leave this summer! I'm only here because you are!"

"Sure you are. While it's quiet back in the barnyard, but you hear one quack and you go running home to Mother Goose."

"Well what do you expect me to do! I can't turn my back on her! She's my mother!"

"So she's your mother." He was losing steam. "What am I then?"

I was also losing steam. And my migraine was going away. "My own true love. You always were. From day one."

"Do you get migraines with me?"

"No."

We sort of curled up and huddled for comfort. We were both beat. "It tears me up," he said, "when I see you feeling like this."

"So why didn't you just give me a little tea and sympathy then?"

"Because I'm not going to sympathize with your craziness. Either you live with me or you don't live with me. My stomach can't stand all this anxiety. I'll probably get an ulcer from you. I can't stand it when you keep running home and getting sick. I can still see you in the hospital that day, all bloody from your sister."

"Why didn't you just tell me how you felt, then?"

"If you don't know how I feel by now you'll never know."

"Can you give an inch and just sympathize a hair and say I love you or something."

"If you believed I love you I'd never have to say it. And if you don't believe it I could say it a thousand times and it wouldn't mean anything. So what is it, me or them."

I kissed him about a hundred times. My head cleared. My eyes cleared. Veils lifted. There was my wonderful world, my tiger and my fish, my star room and the place my heart was. "I guess I'm still dumb," I said. "But I'm not so dumb I don't know you can't go home again."

"I hope you mean it." He was worn out and I was worn out. But we had survived.

"Anyhow I guess I'm home now."

He moved closer and spoke softer. "Don't say it if you don't mean it."

"I *mean* it," I said. "I *mean* it."

We lay back in the forests of the heart, under the stars of our particular sky. Arachne built the web, thread by silken thread.

That was the day I really left Momma. I didn't see her again until almost Christmas.

Chapter Four

❧

OF COURSE I didn't mean absolutely not see her. What was I going to do, be vindictive? She couldn't help herself. What did she have in the world? What she learned she gleaned from the soap operas and various wise people she met in supermarkets. So was I supposed to blame her? On the other hand, I had to save myself.

So I'd phone her a couple of times a week and I'd drop by when I was sure she was out and I'd leave her little notes and pots of ivy and when she asked me to dinner, I told her about the terrible paper that was due or the test I had tomorrow. "I'm going to graduate college and make you proud," I said. It was really wretched, but she had Shera and Shera was blooming, so I had my golden days.

We were free. I learned to play the guitar and Jason took up the recorder and we played shaky duets and we took a course in gemstones and went on field trips hunting for agates, which we never found, but it didn't make any difference, and I started my first series of sonnets. *Sister,* whispered Elizabeth Barrett Browning. Jason lay with his head in my lap and listened as I read:

> *Capturing the fecund heart in flight,*
> *Peonies against the veils of night.*

"Should I change my name when I become well known?" I asked. " 'Molly' is so drab."

"Can't you just write a few poems without being famous?"

"Why shouldn't I be famous?" I said. "I'm swimming in the stream of my destiny." Anyhow it wasn't a matter of fame. That would come when it would come. It was just that I was doing it. Everything, I mean. I drifted, writing a couple of novels in my head. Anyhow I would wear the mantle of my fame lightly. I wouldn't get depressed and stick my head in the oven like Sylvia Plath or jump off a bridge like John Berryman. I would walk with humility. *Good show,* said Shakespeare.

Momma called me just before the Christmas break. "This is ridiculous. Do you know how long it is since you've been to the house?"

"I *know,*" I said. "I'm dying to come. Only I've got quarter finals."

"You had quarter finals last month," said Momma. "Come home."

"I'll just run home for an hour," I said to Jason. "She sounds really grim."

He was slogged down doing his big paper on quantum-something-or-other. "Don't blame me," he said, "if you come back with a nervous breakdown. Don't ask me for sympathy."

"From Momma? She can't affect me now," I said.

"I have aesthetic distance. I understand her. I'm going to write her up as the most unforgettable character I ever met. I'll be back with all the cute stories."

"Dreamer," he said.

For the first time Momma didn't launch into me. She just flicked around the room nervously, picking brown leaves off the ivy. "What are you upset about? I'm here. I'm okay. I even gained a couple of pounds."

"I'm not worried about your weight. I can see how you are. It's Shera."

"What's up?" I said. "I thought everything was super cozy over here."

"Brian makes 'demands' on her. You know what I mean. If you don't want your sister to have internal problems in her later life, please have a talk with Brian."

"You didn't call me over here to talk about my sister's gynecology. Why are you coming down on Brian so hard all of a sudden?"

"Because he has a family," she said. "A rich family. Did you know he had money in the family? And his sister has graciously offered him a place in the business. And he's turned his nose up at it."

"Well that's no surprise. Shera said he hated his sister."

"A poor boy with a wife and a child can't afford to hate a rich sister!"

We heard them at the door, the lovers of the Western World. Such laughter, so happy. Brian paused at the door to kiss her sweet head as he took off her coat, and she kissed his dear cheek. They entwined, like Momma's ivy. "Hello, the lovers!"

"Molly! You're here!" She waddled over to kiss me. Then she remembered she was carrying ice cream so she went into the kitchen to dish it out. And of course Brian went with her so that she wouldn't strain herself lifting the spoons.

"What on earth are you feeding her, she got so big. She's not even five months yet."

"Two brilliant children," said Momma. "This one throws her life away on a nothing artist, and that one lies to me while she's smiling."

"What are you talking about?"

"Don't ask me. I'm only her mother. You're her sister. If you cared about her, you'd come around once in a while to ask what's happening."

Shera and Brian came in with the ice cream. Momma and I sat over untouched plates while Shera and Brian fed each other little spoonfuls. Then Momma said wouldn't the sisters like to have a nice talk and she left to play bingo with Mrs. Casamira. Shera kissed her sweet Brian and begged him to watch some football on TV while she had a heart-to-heart with her sister whom she hadn't seen in a thousand years. They spent five minutes kissing it over, and then Shera pulled me into the bedroom.

It was still her old bedroom, with her pillows and her dolls. She made a place for me and we curled up with the old candy box. "I'm so glad to see you here," she said.

"Shera," I asked, "what month are you in?"

She tugged at a coil of her hair and she sucked a candy. She shrugged her shoulders.

"What does the doctor say?"

"Him," she said. "What does he know?"

"What do you *mean* what does he know? You weren't when you met Brian! You *couldn't* be!"

"*Please* keep your voice down," she said anxiously. "I don't know. I just don't know."

I controlled my voice to a hoarse whisper. "How could you not know a thing like that?"

"It was all so crazy then. I just didn't know! Everything was happening so awful. Momma wasn't being proud of me and all the good things were happening to you and everybody at school was saying 'so she's

Molly's sister' and I was mixed up with all those boys. I just didn't know anything. I love Brian. Please Molly, *help* me."

"Oh Jesus Mary," I said. "You haven't told him yet?"

She was horrified. "I'm not going to tell him! I'm never going to tell him. I never want him to know I wasn't perfect and all."

"Well exactly how are you going to keep this cat in the bag, Shera?"

"I've been eating a lot," she said. "He thinks I'm getting fat. He calls me his dear little piglet. I could have a preemie or something. It happens."

"But that wouldn't be fair to Brian! He's been so straight with you through all this. He loves you. You can't keep it from him!"

"Well what's fair to me?" she said. "I'm the one who's suffering with the baby and all! I'm the one who gets sick in the morning and has gas and everything. It might be his. I just don't know!"

"Look, Shera," I said. "He loves you. Just lay it out to him. He'll understand."

"What do you mean he'll understand? How will he understand? Even I don't understand. You think everybody is like your poetry, well they're not. I'll have a preemie. It will work out. It has to work out. This is the first good thing in my life. They wouldn't give me this one good thing and then take it away again? If I lose Brian, I might as well die."

"How coudd she?" I said to Jason. "How could she pull a stunt like that on Brian? I'd never do a thing like that to you."

"Lie to me?" said Jason. "You're not capable."

"I mean tie you down like that. Like Gulliver."

"Go ahead," he said. "Tie me down."

"I never would," I said. "Not when you haven't even explored the possibilities of your art yet and when we haven't even seen the wild streets of Tangiers and had our time to lie naked on the rocks of Corfu like Henry Miller and follow the sun."

"What art?" he said. "I told you I gave that up. I made my peace with it."

"No you didn't," I said. "You're just waiting to finish your units because you're compulsive. You haven't even begun to paint. Just look at the mural."

"I copy out a picture on a studio wall and that makes me Gauguin?"

"Sure," I said. "Why not?"

"Or I could just be a math teacher someplace in Colorado."

"Then you'll be a brilliant math teacher. You'll think up some new theorem, like Hallem's Law. Numbers are wonderful and mysterious. I never understood numbers. You can conjure with numbers. You can turn base metal into gold."

"You don't listen," he said. "I said math *teacher*, like with a briefcase of papers under my arm."

"Then you'll be Socrates, walking the halls and teaching philosophy with your equations."

"It's a good thing you found somebody like me," he said. "Somebody to hold the kite string while you go flying off into space."

"We'll both fly off," I said. "How many miles to Betelgeuse? How do you find infinity?"

We were warm and cozy and at peace. "I don't see it as Gulliver," said Jason. "I see it as two animals in a jungle burrowed in for a long cold winter. I build the fire, you fix the coconuts and read me poems about peonies and veils of night."

"There is no winter for us," I said. "We'll follow the sun."

"Like two safe animals," he said. "And the storm outside, but who cares because we have everything we need right here."

I tried to pick up the fantasy of the blue men of the Saraha I was thinking of including in a story I was intending to write. But Hamlet kept tugging at my consciousness. He walked up to the castle gate with his briefcase under his arm and a corduroy jacket over his doublet. Ophelia opened the door with a couple of children tugging at her gown. *I never get out of the castle anymore. Did you bring the spices for dinner? The parsley, sage, rosemary and thyme? Sorry,* Hamlet said, *forgot. Stopped at the gym to work out.* He poked at his paunchy stomach. *Oh, that this too too solid flesh would melt . . .*

This is too silly, said Scarlett O'Hara. *Fiddle-de-de A'm tired. A'll think about it tomorrah.*

So would I. Tomorrow.

I would have thought about it during the Christmas break, but it was so wonderful to be free for a couple of weeks, and the whole celebration was not being alone. We both remembered spooky Christmases and this one wasn't. We bought a little live tree and set it in front of the tiger. We combed the foggy beaches for decorations, shells and other marvels washed up by the tide. Or we'd bring our guitar and recorder down to the beach and play carols for people. Or we'd just sit on the sand, wrapped in a big blanket against the chill, and feel lucky.

Jason had to take Christmas dinner with his old aunt in Pomona, and I had to spend some time with Momma and Shera. We could have talked about it after that, but we were indulging ourselves by going to the movies every night and sleeping until noon, and then it was New Year's Eve and we slept the whole night on the beach waiting for magic stars. "This is the best year of my life," said Jason.

"This is the first year of my life," I said, "and I'm ready to see the whole world. We'll go to Europe as soon as you finish in June." I listened to the heart of the ocean and dreamed.

"I thought maybe we might do some camping up in Canada," said Jason. "I've got to get a job for September."

"You don't need a job in September," I said. "Let's buy a one-way flight and stay a year."

He pulled the blanket tighter against the night air. "Warm enough?" I was warm, all the way to the heart. Then he laughed. "Can't you just see us in Paris? You playing the guitar and me drawing sidewalk pictures?"

He thought that was very funny. I didn't think it was funny, I thought it could work. But then we got so comfortable waiting for the year to turn. His heart beating and my heart beating and the beating of the waves. You sort of fall into the rhythm. We slept until the sun came up.

We spent New Year's Day just drifting and reading. The weather was dampish, so we curled up in bed with all the blankets and sandwiches and doughnuts and read and held hands. I was reading a diary of Wordsworth's sister. I got really upset with Wordsworth running all over the place leaving his poor sister, who dreamed up half the stuff he wrote about, stuck home in that damp little house getting chilblains and diarrhea. I was really worried about how they washed all that heavy linen by hand and dried it in the damp weather.

And then we got stuck with the winter quarter. And Jason got a T.A. job, which kept him doing papers practically all night.

It was mid-February when Momma phoned me. "Come quick," she said. "Your sister is having a pree-mie."

"So much for the question of the year," said Jason.

Brian was absolutely berserk. "Was it me?" he asked. "Did I make too many demands on her?"

"Nature made demands," I said. "Babies come. Why aren't you on the way to the hospital?"

"If anything happens because of me . . ."

Momma came out wringing her hands and looking daggers at Brian. "You know who's to blame for this," she said.

"Will you *please* lay off Brian," I hissed.

Shera sat at the edge of the bed, in pain. "You have to make Brian understand," she begged me. "I love him so much. They wouldn't give me this one wonderful thing in my life and then take it away again, would they Molly?"

"He'll understand. Go have yourself a beautiful baby."

"Make him understand. Swear. Swear you'll help me."

"Don't be silly. You're probably having two-minute pains. Get out of here."

"Swear!"

"All right! I swear!"

"God is listening," she said.

We got her to the hospital, don't ask me how. She moaning, Brian almost fainting, Momma accusing. When they took her out of Brian's hands and put her in the wheelchair, we had to get him a glass of water to keep him from passing out.

The three of us sat in severe discomfort in the waiting room. I held Brian's clammy hand and tried to conjure up Tennyson or some other more boring poet to calm me down. Then the nurse came in and told us that Shera had delivered a fine son.

Brian was undone. "Is she all right then? Will the baby live?"

The nurse was perplexed. "Why shouldn't the baby live? Eight and a half pounds. I should say so."

"It's big enough to survive then?"

"They don't come much bigger," said the nurse.

Then Brian was perplexed. "You mean that eight and a half isn't a preemie?"

She was momentarily puzzled, then she was smart. "Well you can see the mother in the recovery room. She's asking for you."

Brian hovered in shock, half dazed, his whole life drifting before his eyes. "Eight and a half isn't a preemie, is it?"

Momma came at him in a fury. "What are you saying about my daughter? Why aren't you running to thank her for giving you a son? Big babies run in this family! Shera was almost twelve pounds, so was Molly. Thank your luck this was a preemie, a full term would have torn her up. When you come to your senses, you beg my forgiveness for what you just said about my child!"

Brian was confused. He looked to me for confirmation. "I trust you, Molly. You tell me the truth."

"We make big babies in our family. I was over twelve pounds, so was Shera. Momma's right. Full term would have torn her, she's so small."

He almost cried in relief. He kissed Momma's hand and begged her forgiveness. When she deigned to forgive him, he ran to see Shera.

Momma dampened her handkerchief in the water fountain and dabbed at her face. "Well that's that," she said.

I was shocked at myself. I couldn't believe what I'd done. "I lied to him."

"You did it for him as well as her," said Momma. "Now forget it. She has her baby now. Here's where the music starts."

Of course it had to be done. There was nothing else for it. "It's her music. Leave her alone now."

"If we left her alone," said Momma, "where would she be now?"

"I lied," I said to Jason. "Without batting an eye, without sweat on my lip. I just lied to him."

"Why on earth did you do it?"

"What do you mean why? She's my sister."

"So that makes her more valuable than Brian? What about your family of man?"

"Let's not discuss this," I said. "You're not rational on the subject of my sister."

"And you are," he said. "I think it's time I got you out of here before something worse happens."

"We'll get out of here by summer so let's not talk about it, okay?"

"I got a job for September," he said.

"Why do you need a job? Why can't we just drift with the sun? We've been stuck in this routine all year."

"The sun only shines in summer. Winter comes. And we're growing out of this place. I have to take a job. And this buddy of mine is opening a private school for bright kids. He asked me to teach the math. For a year anyhow. We can sock away some dough and then we'll take a proper trip."

"A job where? Here in L.A.?"

"I wouldn't leave you here in L.A. if my life depended on it. The school is in Lawrence, Kansas."

"Kansas!"

"Jobs are hard to find now. That's all I can get on short notice."

"But what on earth is in Kansas?"

"Corn. Wheat. You can go to school in Kansas. Or write your great American novel in Kansas." I think he was a little disappointed. "I'll be in Kansas, dammit, that's what will be in Kansas."

"Hey," I said, "I'm sorry. I just got taken by surprise, that's all."

"And we'll have to get married before we leave. It's a family-type town and I figured you'd want a wedding and I suppose you'll die if your sister doesn't come."

"Married!"

A small ice age drifted in from the north.

Jason came out of it sort of startled. "Didn't you expect to get married?"

"You never mentioned married. I never asked you for married. I can love you all right without the little paper. I don't need the official confirmation."

"Well I do!" he said. "I'm not a kite-flyer like you are! I need to know the fixed points! I just assumed that you knew we'd get married!"

"You never talked about it, that's all!"

"Well who needed to talk about it! It was assumed! I mean, did you expect me to get down on my knees after all this time and do the whole romantic bit?"

I was too shocked to answer.

And he got upset and started to pace around. "You never expected to get married? What are you doing here then? Having a little literary romantic fling or something? Is that what you're doing?" He went to the closet and pried out my suitcase. "Get out then! If that's all you're doing, then clear out now!"

I carried the suitcase back to the closet. "You couldn't pry me out of here with a shoehorn. But *married* just came as a shock, that's all. I wasn't ready for it."

The steam went out of the argument. "You really scared me. You did want the whole romantic proposal and everything. I should have known."

"No," I said, "it's okay, really."

"I'm sorry, Molly. I was so busy with my schoolwork, and it scared me to death every time you went home to your family. I'm sorry. I'm really sorry. That was a hell of an insensitive thing to do to you." He bent on one knee, Victorian style. "Can I have your hand in marriage then?"

"Don't be crazy," I said. "You've already got my hand and my heart and my pancreas and everything else."

"Okay, then. So it's set. You'll love it in Kansas. Real Americana."

Dorothy and Toto skipped along the yellow brick road singing, *Tra-de-la, I'm off to see the Wizard.* Why don't you cut this out, I said. I'm getting too old for it. *Hey,* said Dorothy, *so am I. I've grown out of these shoes and my dog is getting too old to leap around, but tell me frankly, how do I get out?*

Arachne smiled and kept spinning. *Don't you know about webs?* she said. *They go two ways, ensnaring both the spinner and the spinee.*

I phoned Momma to see how Shera was getting along. "It's a beautiful baby," said Momma. "A gorgeous baby. But she's worn out and Brian won't leave her side. Who do you think will get stuck with it?"

Chapter Five

❦

BEWARE OF the Ides of March if you live in a converted grocery store. It was so damp, we were almost mildewed. So Jason caught the flu and I caught the flu. I mean it was still love, but we coughed at each other a lot. And he was going crazy with some paper he hadn't finished and I was getting sick and tired of picking the eyebrows out of Julius Caesar and trying to probe the social consciousness of Titus Andronicus, which is a ghastly play. All I wanted to do was curl up with a cup of tea and work on my sonnets. My peonies and veils of night. So I did such a dumb thing. I sent the poems to a magazine. I didn't expect to get them published or anything. I wasn't that foolish. I just expected a note saying, *I am truly astonished at this much talent in someone so young.* I must have been flu crazy. I got back a mimeographed rejection and a note reading: TRY US AGAIN IN TEN YEARS.

"Bastards," said Jason.

My voice was hoarse with anguish and catarrh. "Don't ever mention it again," I rasped. "It was dumb and juvenile. I'm embarrassed to death to think I sent it in."

"Don't be hard on yourself," he said. "I love the veils of night."

"How can I write anything *but* peonies," I said, "when I haven't even seen Tangiers or the goats of Cyprus or Byzantium."

Jason coughed around for a while. The Kleenex had run out and his nose was red from using paper napkins on it. "You mean I'm keeping you from Byzantium."

"Please don't be awful when I feel awful," I said. "You always get terrible when I feel wretched. Don't do that, please."

He fixed himself some tea and dropped the cup and cut his finger and he got testy and wouldn't let me see it to wrap it up, he just put a paper napkin around it. "I heard what you said," he rasped. "Every time reality hits you in the face, you run off to Byzantium. I thought you grew out of those childish fantasies. *Byzantium* . . ." He laughed, or maybe he was just hacking, I couldn't tell.

"Hey," I said, "since when are my dreams just childish fantasies?"

"Let's not have words," he said, coughing up phelgm. "All that lying around naked on the rocks of Corfu. You know what's on the rocks of Corfu? Tourists are on the rocks of Corfu."

"Metéora, then. Where they lift the monks up in baskets."

"Now they have elevators," he said. "And when you come down they put a bumper sticker on your car: *I've been to Metéora to See the Monks in Baskets.*"

"You know what I *mean*, Jason. I'm talking figuratively, not literally. I mean tasting the world. I mean Byzantium."

"Byzantium has been gone for thousands of years,

Molly. There's nothing but shoe stores in Byzantium, and I have a quiz in the morning and don't you think it's time that Pippa grew up? Look at the world as it is for a change."

Long hostile silence while I cleared my larynx enough to speak. "You mean that I've missed the boat."

"Don't put words in my mouth," he said.

"Hey," I said, "it's okay. If it's the truth, then it's good for me to know it. My dreams are cotton candy, that's what you said."

Already he was sorry. We were both sorry and edgy and we hadn't taken enough vitamin C or slept enough. But we got stuck in the groove.

"I didn't mean it the way it sounded," he said.

"That's okay," I said. "I'm very perceptive. I read between the lines. Just forget it."

So we both forgot it.

"Will you come over, please?" begged Shera. "I'm dying over here."

"I'll just run over for an hour," I said to Jason. "To see the baby."

"Can't you pass the baby this time?" he said. "I need a paper typed."

"I'll be back early and I'll fix dinner and I'll do the paper and I'll wash the floor and I'll polish the tiger. Okay?"

"Why are you still sore?" he said.

"Who's sore? Just forget it."

He caught me by the hand and wouldn't let me leave. "Who wants to trample on your dreams? Fly if you want to, but somebody has to keep an eye on the ground."

"Good," I said, "just look up from your tunnel."

He let go of my hand.

"I'm sorry," I said. "I didn't mean that. I'm just still moldy from the rain. Let's forget it."

So we forgot it.

Shera was back in her room, just like the old days, with her dolls and her pillows and her candy. Momma had the baby. "It's like this day and night. She doesn't let me put my hands on him. She even sleeps with the baby in her room because she's afraid he might die of crib death or something."

"He's your baby," I said. "Just take him."

"You try it. You know Momma, how she gets because she's working her fingers to the bone, et cetera."

"This is totally ridiculous," I said. Momma was in the bathroom, bathing that fantastic baby. Some ball of sweet fatness. I bent to kiss his stomach. Delicious little pig. "Why isn't Shera bathing her baby?" I asked her.

"She's getting back her strength," said Momma. "Do you think this is easy on the back? Just try it."

"Her back is stronger than yours. Give her the baby."

"Do you think I like the extra work?" she said. "I pick up after her day and night."

"Let her pick up after herself then."

I heard Brian dragging in. He came hesitantly into the bathroom to kiss the baby, he took one look at Momma and ran.

"His sister offered him the job of the century," said Momma, raising her voice about a thousand decibels so that he could hear it, "and he *turned up his nose at it! A man with a wife and child to feed!*"

I could hear Shera and Brian arguing in the bedroom. What a mess. I knocked at the bedroom door. Brian was slumped in a chair, looking miserable. Shera held her calico doll to her face, which was streaked from crying.

"You explain it to her," said Brian. "She knows I hate my sister. I'll die and roast in hell before I take a penny from her."

"You took the wedding silver all right," said Shera, "so why is the job so different?"

"I only took the silver because you wouldn't give it back, Shera. Talk to her," he begged me. "A buddy of mine offered us a place at the beach while he's out of town. I want to get her and the baby out of here, but she won't go."

"It's not a place," she said. "it's a dumpy room with a kitchen and a tiny bedroom and we wouldn't even have a TV or anything."

"It's not a dump," said Brian. "She could have fresh air for her and the baby. It's only until June. I'll have a full-time job in June."

"You know how the beach gets at night," said Shera, "with the murderers and the rapists and all."

"Those are Casamira rapists," I explained to Brian.

"I have a baby!" she said. "I can't just get stuck out there with nobody!"

"Since when am I nobody?" said Brian angrily.

"He's right," I said to Shera. "It's beautiful to live at the beach. You can hear the waves all night."

"Why are you taking his side?" flared Shera.

"Since when are you lovebirds on sides?"

"It's your mother," said Brian. "She wants to leave your mother but she's scared to death."

"That's not true!" said Shera. "If you took your sister's job, we could have a regular place by now."

"Shera," said Brian, "I will cut my throat before I take one goddamn cent from my sister!"

"Enough!" I said. "This is rot and super rot!" I marched into the kitchen where Momma had the baby in the carriage, rocking him while she fixed dinner. I started to wheel the baby back to Shera's room.

"Where are you going?" she said. "He just fell asleep."

"This is her baby," I said, "not your baby. If you want a baby, go have one."

"Smart mouth," said Momma. "Tell her to be careful of the way she holds his back."

I settled the baby in Shera's arms. She snuggled against the pillows and kissed her own baby. Brian put an arm around her and took the baby's hand. "Honey," he begged, "please let's get out of here. You'll love it at the beach. It won't be that bad."

She leaned against him. "I'm scared to be with the baby alone and all."

"With me, honey? You're scared with me?"

She worried, she frowned, she looked at me desperately.

"It's your life," I said. "Do you want to live it here with Momma?"

I could see that she was frightened. She hugged her baby. And her dolls. And her old familiars. "Okay," she said. "What about my things?"

"I'll pack your things and bring them over later. Just get out of here."

"Momma's going to be so mad with me," said Shera. "Tell her I love her."

They were out the door and gone. The car drove off.

Then Momma came out of the kitchen, drying her hands on a dishtowel. "Dinner is ready. Where is everybody?"

"Sit down," I said.

She sniffed around, she smelled trouble. "Where are they?"

"Gone. They've eloped."

"What have you done?" she said to me.

"She's left for her own place, Momma. You knew it had to happen sooner or later."

"And you let her do this thing? You let your sixteen-year-old sister go off to some shack on the beach with a newborn baby? If something terrible happens from this, you'll know who to blame!"

"I know," I said. "I'm also to blame for the sinking of the *Titanic,* and the murder of the Archduke Ferdinand at Sarajevo. Momma, I never told her to have a baby. I argued with her and I argued with you. But she wanted it and she got it. So please let them live their own life now."

Momma fell into a chair, defeated. "I had two gems

of daughters. I tried to make it better for them than it was for me."

"She has Brian now," I said. "She got what she wanted."

"You struggle and you struggle," she said, "and in the end it all comes out the same."

I just didn't feel like going back to the studio yet, that's all. I needed air and space, and, I think, stars. It was lunar, really lunar, this fat-faced moon that spotlighted the whole Venice night, that hit the water and broke the surface into dancing points. From somewhere I heard children singing. *Needles and pins, needles and pins, when a man marries his trouble begins.* Maybe they weren't singing that. But Brian was on needles and pins, wasn't he. When was *married* not trouble? It was for Momma and it was for Shera.

A guy and a girl passed me. They were having an argument. She wore a bikini and it was really cold. I wondered why she didn't get dressed before coming outside. He held a transistor radio, listening to it as they walked, even though she was trying to talk to him. She kept yelling about something and asking him to turn it off, but he just turned up the sound. She pounded at his arm but he pushed her away. So she pulled the radio out of his hands and smashed it on the cement. He stood there so astonished, being sorry for himself and his radio. And she stood about a pace away, shivering with cold, almost ready to cry. He never even looked over to where she was.

Then a man came along with a monkey on a leash. I asked him about the monkey but he said it was an ape. It walked its apelike gait over benches and along the ground and finally it jumped up on his shoulder. He was a sort of nothing guy but all sorts of people came to ask him about his monkey that was an ape, so he was happy.

Then a drunk hassled me for a quarter and I gave it

to him. He was so astonished he asked me for a dollar.

Somewhere in my head a voice said, *All this is happening here? So what's happening in Istanbul?*

Jesus Mary, Shera had got married and she was stuck at sixteen. And Momma had been stuck all her life! I was eighteen and I was loved, but love was supposed to be as wide as the heart was wide. I had only just come out of a snail shell; I didn't want to go live in a tunnel!

But I couldn't live without Jason! I got scared, really scared. I ran back to the studio. Pure panic. As I climbed the stair-ladder, I heard the halting staccato of my typewriter. I'd forgotten his paper. He sat hunched over the typewriter, working two-fingered. He didn't even look up.

I rushed around the place in a fit of guilt, cleaning up, washing the dishes that were piled in the sink, taking down his socks that were drying over the heater, rolling them up.

"Leave the damn socks alone," he said. "I never asked you to do my socks. Go write a play or something."

"Socks exist," I said. "Socks are reality." I put the socks in his drawer. I was tired to the bones. I was tired of Shera's problems and Momma's problems and everybody's problems. *In Istanbul a woman in a flowered pantaloon was sitting up against a tree looking at the clear sky, watching the stars.*

I was just going to close the drawer when I saw them. My poems. My dumb peonies and veils of night that I had crumpled and tossed. He must have retrieved them from the wastebasket and straightened them and kept them. My *poems.* He loved my poems. He'd probably eaten dinner out of a can and he'd probably worried about me all evening. And there he was bent over the typewriter with his two-finger typing, which he *hated.* If the enemy ever captured him to make him give up secrets, they would sit him

in front of a typewriter and make him type a paper
two-fingered. I shoved him away. "I'll finish it."

"Don't do me any favors," he said sullenly.

"Why shouldn't I do you favors?" I said.

He yielded me up the typewriter and while I typed
he made me tea, and when the paper was finished we
tried to squeeze into the window seat to drink and
watch the street, but we had swelled or something and
it felt tight. "This place is getting too small for us," he
said. "The paint is peeling off the tiger. He looks as if
he's molting." Down the street a couple of kids came
by on skateboards. They did some fancy turns and
then swung around the corner. We could hear their
laughter drifting back on the silence. "I don't like
what's happening to us," said Jason.

"Nothing is happening to us."

"We're starting to molt, like the tiger."

"We could dry out in Morocco," I said.

"You know I'm getting sick and tired of your running off to Morocco every time we have a problem,"
he said. "Not Salt Lake City or Memphis, Tennessee,
but someplace you can't get to, like Timbuktu or Mar-
rakech. Okay, I'll call you on it. We'll go to Byzantium. As soon as the last test is over."

"Are you *serious?*" I screamed. "We'll hop a
freighter and drop off on Mykonos and bake in the
sun?"

"I'll sell the car and we'll buy a couple of charter
tickets to Europe and we'll backpack and stay in
hostels."

"Who wants you to sell the car?" I said. "It's your
only prized possession in the world! You love that ancient classic rattletrap!"

"Well I love you more," he said.

"But I don't want you to have to make any big
sacrifice for me."

"Why shouldn't I make a sacrifice? What do you
think love is anyhow? You want Sydney Carton, you've

got Sydney Carton. Now do you want us to go or don't you?"

"Of course I want us to go, but I want us to have a voyage of the spirit, the way we've been living here. You know what I mean by following the sun!"

"When you follow the sun you still have to sleep and find breakfast and locate johns and have your passport stamped."

"We'll sleep under the stars and we'll eat in sidewalk cafés."

"In Istanbul? You get dysentery from sidewalk cafés in Istanbul. And when was the last time you slept under the stars with crawlies in your hair?"

"You'll teach me then. We'll sleep side by side, under the sky, the way we do here."

"Here we have a roof. So is it yes or no?"

"Of course it's yes, but not like this, with all the romance out of it."

"If there's romance, you'll find it. Meanwhile, we'll have to sell the car and find a charter flight, you have to get a passport, and if you're thinking of eating in Istanbul, you'll have to take shots."

"For what?"

"They have cholera in Byzantium. For once I want you to see reality. I'll drag you through so many underdeveloped countries, you'll have local color coming out of your ears."

This was not what I meant. This was not what I meant at all. I tried to fall asleep to the fantasy of soft Mediterranean sounds and the slushing of water. All I heard was Jason snoring slightly from the postnasal drip he got sleeping in the damp studio.

Shera phoned me from the beach apartment. "I love it here! I never was so happy in all my life!"

"She's happy," I said to Jason. "I knew she'd work it out."

"Today," said Jason. "This morning."

"What," I asked him, "have you got against my sister?"

"Will you come over *please?*" said Shera. "I'm dying."

She had little Brian propped up, feeding him carrots. They dribbled down his chin and onto his stomach but he seemed to be enjoying it. He burbled with laughter and kicked his feet. "I'm not very good at this yet," she said.

"So what are you dying about?"

"Brian got his job finally."

"That's marvelous."

"It's in *Ore*gon."

"You'll love Oregon. It's beautiful in Oregon. They don't litter and the air is clean."

"I'm not going off to any crazy wild place with a new baby," she said.

"Since when is Oregon crazy and wild?" I smelled a rat. "Has Momma been over?"

"No," she protested. "Yes," she admitted. "Only when I get swamped. But she's right about that. What if the baby gets sick up there and I don't have anyone? Brian's sister offered him a wonderful job. Why can't he just take it for a year, until we get a better car and the baby is older or something?"

"Because he hates his sister."

"So do I," she said, opening the baby's applesauce. "She's such a bitch. But we all have to do things we don't like. We're married and all. It's not any fun taking care of a baby day and night without even a washer-dryer or anything. What if the baby gets sick in the middle of some desert or on an empty road." She ran a finger over the soft fuzz of the baby's head. "I'm scared, Molly. What if Brian runs out on me and I'll be stuck up there alone?"

"Why on earth should Brian run on you? He's crazy about you."

She bent to kiss the baby. "Sometimes he's not. And he hates his sister more than he loves me."

"That's crazy."

"Well he does. How do I know he really loves me and all? Unless I know for sure, I'm afraid to go."

"Why don't you just go and find out? If anything happens just call me or Momma."

"Then you think something *will* happen," she said nervously.

"I only said *if*, Shera. For contingencies."

"Please don't use words I don't understand. And you'll probably be off with Jason someplace and I'd die before I'd call Momma. She'd say I-told-you-so for the rest of my life. I have to know for certain if he loves me."

"Like how?" I asked.

She hefted the baby on her stomach and lay there hugging him. "I'll find out," she said.

"Don't do anything dumb," I said.

"I'll find out."

How did I get so far behind in my work? Jason took over all the household chores and made me a neat schedule and sharpened all my pencils and filled my pens, which he said was a waste of time but I couldn't stand ballpoints, I needed to see the true flow of ink. The only thing we didn't do was take the phone off the hook.

"I'm stuck here at the shop," said Brian. "I can't get home until ten. I tried to call Shera because she worries if I'm a minute late but nobody answers out there. She never takes the baby out at night. I hate to ask you . . ."

"I'll run over," I said.

"You'll run over where?" asked Jason.

"Brian's worried because nobody answers at the apartment. I'll just run over and see if everything is okay."

"The hell you will. You'll never finish tonight as it

is. Leave your sister alone. She's got a husband to take care of her."

"It's just for a minute. She's stuck out there alone with the baby."

"It's her *alone* and it's her *baby,* Molly!"

"You stay here. I'll go."

"She'll go . . . she'll go." He fussed so much I wished he'd stayed behind. "Your sister is some pain in the ass," he said.

The apartment was locked. The living room was dark. But there was a small light in the bedroom. I knocked at the bedroom window. Nobody answered.

"She's not home," said Jason. "This is a wild-goose chase. Let's go."

"Why is the light on, then? I'm nervous about her, the way she's been acting. Please go inside and look around." I made him jimmy open the bathroom window.

"This is ridiculous," he called from inside. He opened the door for me. "You're beginning to act like your mother." As he opened the bedroom door she was framed in a small circle of light from the bedside lamp. She lay across the made-up bed, in her best gown, her hair combed out against the pillow. On the bedside table was an overturned bottle of pills and a note.

"Dear God," I said, "what has she *done!* She's *killed herself!*"

Jason ran to the bed and bent over her. "Not with this heaving bosom she hasn't." He checked the bottle and counted the pills. "Not with this junk. She's having a big sleep and she's going to have a bigger headache." He handed me the note. "Here's a piece of literature for you."

Dere Brian. I cant stand it anymore. If you loved me youd take the job with your sister. If you dont love me I mite as well be dead.

"Why doesn't she wake up then?"

Jason bent over the bed and shook her, not gently. "Shera, get the hell up!"

She stirred, she murmured drowsily and went back to sleep.

"She's unconscious. Call an ambulance."

"That's all she needs," said Jason. "An ambulance and the police department. Go make some coffee." He shook her. She opened her eyes and then closed them. He hefted her up by the armpits and dragged her off toward the bathroom.

"Be gentle with her, please!"

"The next time she pulls a stunt like this," he said, "let her call me first. I'll tell her what to take."

I heard her moaning. I heard Jason swearing. Coffee, where did she keep coffee? Where did she keep anything? What a kitchen. There was practically nothing but baby food in the cupboard. I found some Ovaltine. I made that. I heard her gagging and coughing. I heard the shower and I heard her squeal. Jason brought her out, wet-headed and fighting, and dumped her on the bed. I toweled her soaked hair. I wrapped her in blankets and tried to feed her Ovaltine but she was still gagging. "How could you *pull* a thing like this!" I said to her. "You could have killed yourself. Do you *hear* me, Shera!"

Her eyes were still fogged, but she was coming awake. She tried to focus on the room. "Where's Brian?"

"Working overtime. He asked us to check on you. Where did you dream up this crazy scheme? You could have hurt yourself. Are you okay now?"

"Why isn't Brian here!" she screamed. "Why did you mess in! You should have let Brian come! Now it's all for nothing!" She turned over and wept into a pillow. "Now I'll never know. Now what will I do?"

"Shera," I said, "I could kill you myself. Where's the baby?"

"With Momma," she wept. "Please go get him. And don't tell her. *Please* don't tell her what happened."

"How can the baby be with Momma? Momma's not home."

"She said I could always send the baby over on Monday if I was tired or something. She watches programs on Monday. Just don't tell her, Molly. Don't tell anybody."

"The tube is out of her TV. Momma is with Casamira playing bingo at Our Lady of Sorrows. She called me."

Shera woke up, like ammonia under the nose. "What do you *mean* she's not home! She has to be home! Beebee took the baby there!"

"Who's Beebee?"

"She's my friend! She said she would drive the baby right over to Momma's house!"

"You gave your baby to some *stranger!*"

"She's not a stranger! She's my best friend out here!"

"Doesn't she ever let up?" asked Jason. "Doesn't she take time out for a bath or to read the paper or to watch TV?"

"What we don't need is sarcasm!" I said. "Please go find her baby!"

"Are you sure it was a red brick house?"

"I'm nervous." Shera ran along the beachfront in her robe and slippers. "I can't remember."

"Which red brick house, Shera? Try to think."

"I meet her on the beach all the time and we walk to her red brick house. But it's so dark now."

We ran through three red brick buildings until we saw the baby's carriage in the hallway. "Which apartment?"

She pulled her robe around her. "I don't know *which* apartment. I *told* you, I meet her on the beach."

We rang for the manager. The woman who came

to the door in the flowered muumuu wasn't too happy to see us. "Do you happen to have a Beebee living here?" I asked.

She eyed us suspiciously. "I have a Beebee and a Bowwow and a Booboo. Which one is Beebee?"

"She has my baby," said Shera in distress.

Now the manager was distressed. "I heard a baby crying up there but the girl in that apartment doesn't have a baby. It cried so long I called the police."

I had to hold Shera up to keep her from falling.

"You can't leave a baby alone like that, miss," said the manager. "How did I know whose baby it was?"

In came Beebee, in a bikini, with an armful of groceries. "God," she said, "where *were* you? I tried to take him over to your mother but she wasn't home. And when I got back to your place, nobody answered. Then he got hungry and I went to give him the bottle but I dropped it and it broke so I ran out to the drugstore and the tire blew . . ."

"Where is the baby now?" I asked the manager.

"The police took it."

We had to sit Shera down and put her head between her legs.

She couldn't go to the police station in a bathrobe. We walked her back to the apartment, supporting her between us. She ran into the bedroom to get some clothes. We heard her cry of alarm.

Brian sat on the edge of the bed holding her note.

He looked at us and at the note again and then at Shera. "I was sick worrying about you when Molly didn't call back, so I left the shop and came home. I've been phoning all the hospitals." He held the note out to her. "Is this how you were going to get me to take my sister's job?"

"I didn't!" she said. "I swear!"

"Don't swear to me anymore, Shera." He just walked out.

That poor baby. They had already put him in a shelter home. She tried to explain to them at the station what had happened, that she had left the baby with a friend in an emergency. But she was a juvenile and she had to see the juvenile investigator and by that time she was really upset and she started to faint and we had to bring her water. So I sat with her while Jason explained. They looked over toward her. They made us all wait while they checked to see if she had a record. A record! My sister with a record!

"Make them hurry," she begged. "I have to be home when Brian comes back. He'll be so mad with me."

Jason was furious with Shera. He wouldn't talk to her, he talked to me. "They could have filed charges. This time they're letting her pick up the baby. *Next* time . . ."

"There's not going to *be* a next time," I said, mostly for Shera.

"Please," she begged, "let's get the *baby.*"

He must have screamed for hours. Shera undressed him and inspected him and kissed him and dressed him again and he never woke up. "He's a beautiful baby," said the woman who had taken care of him.

Shera was trying not to cry, but tears ran down her cheeks. "I never left him alone. I never took my eyes off him. It was an accident."

"Accidents are terrible," said the woman. "I hope you watch him better."

We brought her back to the apartment.

Momma was there. "Have fun," she said. "Live your own life. I phoned her when I got home and nobody answered. I came over and the whole place was open. I thought some Manson murderers had killed her."

"Please don't yell anymore," said Shera. "My head hurts."

"You deserve to have your head hurt," I said. "Next time think of the baby."

"All right," said Momma. "Done is done. Pack the baby's things and let's go home."

"I'm staying here," said Shera.

"Over my dead body," said Momma.

"I'm staying," she said. "I want to be here when Brian comes home."

"And if he doesn't come home," said Momma.

"He *is* coming back! Don't *say* he's not!"

"Let her stay," I said to Momma. "It was her fault. Let her make it up with him. I'll stay with her if she wants."

"I don't want," said Shera. "I just want to be left alone!"

"I told her when she came here that this would happen," said Momma. "I warned you both."

"If you hadn't hounded her about Brian's sister, nothing would have happened," I said.

"All right," said Momma, "you take the responsibility. Stay alone," she said to Shera. "If you need help, ask your sister."

She wouldn't let us stay. We went back to the studio but we were up most of the night. I phoned her a couple of times but she asked me not to because she always thought it was Brian and she couldn't stand that it wasn't. And she wanted to go to sleep now.

Jason couldn't sleep either so we got up and made coffee. There was a moon that night and it came into the skylight and softened the room. "Things are getting fuzzy around the edges," I said.

"It will get clearer when you leave L.A."

"It kills me to think of Shera all alone out there on the beach. She must be dying."

"When is your sister not dying?" he asked.

I found her sitting on a bench out near the water. A crazy unseasonal storm had rolled in. Dirt-gray whitecaps peeled like long strippers off the crests of waves. The baby was curled in her lap, bundled to the eyes, one little hand out, playing with the edge of her sweater. The wind caught her hair and feathered it against her face. "It's too cold out here," I said. "Come inside."

She hugged the baby and pulled the sweater around them both. "He has to come back," she said. "He's probably hanging around someplace worrying about me. He'll see that I'm waiting for him. I want him back."

"It looks like rain," I said. "Come inside now."

"I did such a dumb thing," she said. "I know that now. If he comes back I'll go anyplace with him. I just don't want to be alone." The muddy fringes of waves rolled in closer to the shore. "I always mess up, don't I."

"That's not true," I said.

"I hate Jason," she said. "He was so mean to me that time. I wish you weren't stuck with him and all."

"I'm not stuck. Why do you say I'm stuck?"

"*I* know," she said. She looked out at the grayness and the moving clouds and the slate water chopping and slapping against the sand. "They do that," she said. "They make you do what they want or they run on you. Momma was right." She bent to kiss the baby. "It's terrible to have a baby with nobody."

"Do you wish you hadn't?"

"Don't even say it," she warned me. "I don't want any more hard luck than I have." She huddled with the baby against the cold. "You remember that book you used to read to me? About little women? If we were little women, we'd still be girls."

I understood what she meant. She was just sixteen and I was eighteen. Only she was a mother and I was on my way to Byzantium to see the shoe stores and then I'd be settling down in Kansas.

"Do you think Momma was right about everything?" She cradled the baby against her as she watched the turbulent sea.

"Bring her home," said Momma. "She can't stay in that place alone. Do you want me to lie awake night after night worrying about her? And who are all those strange people hanging around?"

"She's managing," I said. "I go by in the morning and you're there in the afternoon. Brian sent her some money but he won't talk to her yet."

"Good riddance to bad rubbish," she said.

"Don't say that. She loves him."

"Don't talk to me about love," said Momma. "Look at these girls. This one is brilliant and throwing her life away, and that one is gorgeous and stuck with a baby and nothing."

"The joke's on you," I said. "I'm probably going to marry Jason, and he's a very substantial man."

"Today," said Momma. "So was Brian. Very substantial. Just look at your sister."

"Wake up," said Jason, rubbing my face and my hands. "You had a nightmare."

I was still shaken. Something was coming in the window.

Then I remembered. Ivy was coming in the window.

I tried to pick up a good fantasy, sailing over the soft clouds and down below the fleet of fishing ships.

"Don't forget to fill in the forms for the passport," said Jason sleepily. "And if you want to do some camping over there, we'll need backpacks."

Hello Captain Ahab! We're headed for wild water! How is it with whales?

He waved his stick at me and hailed me. *Don't forget the Dramamine!* he called.

Chapter Six

❧

"EVERYBODY UP!" said Jason. "It's summer."

The sun was blinding me coming through the skylight, and the tiger was grinning away like crazy, and Jason had put the coffee on, and there was a juice glass full of daisies on the floor beside the bed. He must have gone out to pick them in the vacant lot behind the garage. "What's all this?"

"We're going to be late to class without the car, but the sun is out and the peonies are blooming, so get up and write me a poem or something."

I sat up. I reached for some nice fantasy but there was a cloud cover over my head. "Why am I getting this special treatment?"

He squatted down and rubbed my shoulders, which felt like wrought iron, they were so stiff. "Since when are you having all these nightmares?"

"They came," I said. "I think I have a vitamin de-

111

ficiency, I feel so ragged. You go ahead without me. I want to drop by Shera's anyhow."

"We've got two and a half weeks before takeoff, and you'll never finish your work as it is. So why don't you leave Shera alone for a while?"

"I know," I said, "it's just that it takes the edge off everything that things aren't settled with my sister."

"Since when is anything ever settled with your sister?"

"Please don't start it again," I said.

"I'm not starting anything. Only we've had a sloggy winter and a wet spring, and it's over and I'm getting steamed up myself about the trip."

"Are you? Are you honestly? Not just because I want to go?"

"I want to be anyplace where I can see you draw a nice clean breath again. Now eat your daisies and drink your coffee and let's get to class."

Only I couldn't concentrate. I tried to focus on the page and I saw her alone with the baby and a phone that didn't ring. So I cut my next class and took the bus out to the beach.

The door to the apartment stood open and I heard guitar music. I saw Beebee and another, older version of Beebee sitting on the floor drinking Diet Pepsi, and some guy sitting in the corner strumming the guitar.

Shera was diapering Brian Jr. on the kitchen table. What a handful. He could push himself up on his stomach with his fat arms. He grinned like a maniac. She turned him over to diaper him. He kicked and screamed with delight and grabbed her hair. "He's getting so hard to handle already, he squirms so much and all. I think my back is breaking."

"Anything from Brian?"

"He's around," she said. "Beebee saw him."

"Did you try to call him at work again?"

"He's being awful, Molly. Please, you call him.

Make him come home. I'll die out here alone if I don't have somebody."

"You don't look alone," I said. "Who are all these new people hanging around?"

The baby fussed until she picked him up. "It's just Beebee's sister and Beebee's boyfriend. How long can Brian be awful like this? He wants me to come begging. Well I will beg now if he'll only come home. I don't even know where he's sleeping."

Beebee and her sister, in bikinis with their bones sticking out like victims of Appalachia, sat drinking their Diet Pepsis. The blond boyfriend with the long sun-bleached hair and the single earring strummed some chords, trying to play something by Leonard Cohen but he had the notes wrong.

"Maybe if Brian sees Ralph hanging around," said Shera, "he'll get jealous and come home."

"*Shera,* haven't you been burnt enough with all these tricks?"

"Well what am I supposed to do?" she asked desperately. "His friend is taking the apartment back in June! Everything I try goes wrong. I'll die if I have to go back to Momma. Please find Brian. Tell him how awful I feel and how much I miss him."

"You talk to Brian," I said to Jason. "It wouldn't be right coming from me, but you could talk to him man to man."

"Man to man," said Jason, "I'd tell him to run like hell."

"Don't say that. You don't know how miserable she is."

"Then why should the two of them be miserable? If she gave a damn about Brian, she'd be up in Oregon."

"How can I go off and have myself a good time when she's still suffering?"

"You mean she messes up everything and you have to pay the piper? I haven't got any sympathy for your sister and if you step into that hornet's nest she keeps for herself, you're going to have to deal with me. Okay?"

"Don't be so *macho* about it," I said.

"Somebody has to make sense out of this," he said. "Your thinking is mushy. So I'm thinking for both of us."

"Let her come home," said Momma. "Brian isn't coming back, so she might as well adjust herself."

Mrs. Casamira shuffled the tarot deck and cut it. She showed me the card. The Sun, with two little children basking in its rays. "Time to forgive and forget," she said.

"I tried to tell the two of you but nobody listened," said Momma. "Well done is done. So bring your sister home now."

"She doesn't want to come home," I said. "And I'm leaving in a week myself. I told you that."

"You told me with your eyes," she said. "I see this affair is almost over. I see you coming to your senses."

Mrs. Casamira cut another card for me. The Fallen Tower. "It's this way with women," she said. "We build the tower, we bring the men into it, and then it all comes tumbling down."

I stopped at a pay phone and called Brian at the shop. "If you won't come to see her, come to see us at least."

"Okay," he said.

"This is going to be very touchy," I said to Jason, "so please don't say anything to put him off."

"How could you even think I'd pull something like that?"

"I'm just so desperate," I said, "and I know the way you feel about my sister."

"You're not only desperate, you're getting soft in the head. How would I do anything that could hurt you?"

"I'm *sorry*. I'm not thinking straight. You were right that first time. You should have fallen in love with an orphan. Do you still love me then?"

Brian knocked at the door downstairs. "You pick a super time to talk about love," said Jason.

Brian was hangdog, and I found it hard to be warm and sympathetic. He let Jason pour him a beer but he didn't drink it. He just sat warming the glass with his big hands, not looking at me.

"So what's happening between you lovebirds? Still not singing, I guess."

"I tried to talk with her a couple of times," said Brian. "I've been hanging around there. She stood not ten feet away from me and she wouldn't say anything."

"She probably didn't see you. She's been out of her mind worrying about you."

"She saw me."

"Well you know Shera when she's hurt. She's only sixteen, you knew she was a little childish, so why didn't you speak to her first?"

"Because she has someone else," he said.

"No she hasn't. You mean those people hanging around? The boy is a friend of Beebee's. She's just so lonely out there by herself she can hardly stand it."

"She goes out with him."

"That's not true!"

"Isn't it? I've hung around there at night waiting for her to come home with him. That's how much she cares. I'm not even sure about the baby anymore."

"But you're wrong about the guitar player! She never leaves the baby alone at night anyhow. She wouldn't!"

"You don't know your sister," said Brian. "Tell her . . ." He broke up and couldn't speak at all. As he left he said, "Just tell her good-bye."

"I don't believe it!"

"Sure you don't," said Jason. "You always idealized

your sister. She's a poor defenseless thing. She's more to be pitied than blamed. I told you the truth on day one and you wouldn't believe me."

"I don't believe you now," I said.

"What do you *mean* he came to you!" Shera screamed. "Why didn't he come to me if he had something to say!"

"Why didn't you tell me you saw Brian on the beach? Why didn't you talk to him?"

"It was right after it happened! I wanted to talk to him! I was dying to talk to him! He saw me standing there with my heart hanging out. Then he just walked away."

"Why didn't you call him back?"

"I was scared. I didn't know what to say, that's why. If you did a dumb thing like that, what would you say?"

"Are you going out with that guitar player, that Ralph?"

"No, I'm not!" She bit at the edge of her lip. "I did once."

"*Shera!*"

"Beebee loaned him to me. To make Brian jealous. Brian's friend was taking back the apartment. I thought if I went out with Ralph it would make Brian do something."

"It did," I said. "He left."

"The studio is rented out," said Jason. "They upped the rent because of the tiger, so that makes me a professional. Maybe I'll get some paints and fool around while you're lying naked on the rocks of Corfu."

"How am I going to leave with my sister in this fix?" I said.

"When was your sister not in a fix?"

I had done so many back papers I was seeing quotation marks in front of my eyes. So I went down to the pool to soak the stiffness out of me. I hung at the side, ducking and blowing, letting my legs drift with the eddies of other swimmers. I kept thinking of Shera back there with the baby and me gone someplace.

"Let's see a few laps!" said Giselle. "You're all out of shape."

I couldn't let go of the side of the pool.

Momma had the carriage out for a walk along the beach. Shera and I sat at the Meatless Marathon Hall drinking herb tea and trying to figure it out. "What can I do?" she asked desperately.

"Let's look at your options. You can one, go back to Momma."

"And she'll get my baby forever and I'll be stuck for the rest of my life."

"Two, put your baby in a nursery or something and get yourself a job."

"At what? I never worked before."

"Then three, get on welfare and get your own place."

"It's not enough to live on. Beebee's sister does it. Where would I live? I'm afraid."

"Then all I can think of is four. Maybe you'll have to give up the baby."

"Don't even say a thing like that! I love the baby!"

"Then what else can I do! I'm leaving next week and I can't stand it that you're still floating around not settled."

"Please don't go! Stay with me. Jason's just taking you away to spite me."

"That's not true, Shera. You just don't know Jason."

"I know men," she said. "I know what happened to your father and my father, and I knew Brian. I thought he would love me all my life, he swore on Bibles he would, and look at me now. I could have been in contests and all. Momma was right. She was right about me and she's right about him. Please don't go off God knows where. Stay with me and my baby."

"I'm trying to get you settled before I go," I said.
"So what is it? What do you want to do?"

She stirred more sugar in her tea. "Get on welfare I
guess."

"We'll start looking for a place. And you're all finished with that Ralph guy."

She didn't answer.

"Shera . . ."

"I don't even want him hanging around," she said.
"At first when Brian left I was so hurt. They all run on
me, Molly. I don't know why they run. All those
other boys, when I was being crazy at school, they
made love with me and then when it was finished, they
didn't have anything to say to me. Then Brian ran. At
least Ralph was nice to me, at least somebody wanted
me. Then he started to get weird and all."

"What do you mean 'weird'?"

"Only when he drinks too much."

"Shera, are you letting some weirdo hang around you
and the baby! What's the matter with you? Are you
going to drive me crazy worrying about you?"

"Please don't yell and all. People are listening. I
want to get rid of him. I *tried* to get rid of him, but he
just won't go."

"What do you mean he won't go? Open the door
and kick him out. Just tell him good-bye and good
luck. Do you want me to do it for you?"

"I will," she said.

"Do you want to go back to Momma's just for a few
days until you get rid of him?"

"I can't stand it back there," she said. "She's on me
every minute. You know how she is. I want to make it
on my own, Molly. I really do. Just help me."

"Then kick out the bum first of all. And we'll get
you on county aid and we'll find you a place to live."

"You're the only one I can trust," she said. "You're
the only one who was really good to me. I should have
listened to you before."

"God bless you for helping your sister," said Momma. "I knew you wouldn't run off on this little vacation and leave her in the lurch like this."

"I am leaving," I said. "On Monday. But I'll find her a safe place to live first."

"What's safe?" asked Mrs. Casamira. "Where's safe?"

"Here's what we'll do," said Momma. "Tell her there are no safe apartments for young girls with babies. She'll come back here."

"Just try to find an apartment," said Mrs. Casamira. "My niece in Seattle waited a year for an apartment."

"Did she get it?"

Mrs. Casamira looked to Momma to see if she got it.

"That's what I thought. Leave Shera alone this time. This time she's going to make it."

"What do you mean you failed two tests?" said Jason. "Since when do you fail tests? Try to arrange some make-ups. You can't just throw away a whole quarter."

"I don't have time for make-ups. I'm trying to get her into a therapy group and we're looking for apartments. Can't we change the tickets, just to give ourselves an extra week?"

He almost hit the ceiling. "There's only one three-month charter that will get us back to Kansas in time for the fall semester!"

"Then let's go later and just stay. We'll get a one-way flight on a regular airline . . ."

". . . and work in France and live on the Rive Gauche. I know. Without working papers and with your two years of French. Don't upset me," he said. "The books and the kitchen stuff are going out with my buddy on Sunday afternoon and somebody else is moving in here on Monday morning, so that's it."

"*Who's* moving into our place!"

"Another couple of people in love I guess."

In love. I was caught in a time warp or something.

I got a flash of the old days, those sweet first days. I tried to put myself back, to see the softness in Jason's eyes. I think he was trying to see the softness in mine. We hung on to each other, because if we didn't, we might just walk off into the jungle and get lost behind the trees. I think we were scared to death. "Right now I wouldn't mind some fixed points," I said. "I feel as if I'm free-floating and I'm losing my planet."

"Just answer me one thing," he said. "Without thinking."

"That's not hard," I said. "I haven't been thinking for some time."

"Do you love me?"

I tried to drift back, to get the feel of it again, the tender sweetness, the way we lay on the beach and breathed in the night together, the way we sat two hours over a sea urchin in the tide pools, watching and holding hands. "You're my morning and my evening star," I said. "I doubt if I'll ever love anyone else."

"Then trust me. I'll get you out of here if I have to wrap you in a rug like Cleopatra and carry you out. I'll take you into every freaky corner of the Càsbah. I'll even stand back a couple of paces and I won't disturb your spontaneity unless somebody is trying to cut your throat or something."

"Who's going to cut my throat in a shoe store?"

"Well some shoe salesmen are more sensitive than others. I'm not kidding you, Molly. We had something so good. It's all gone sour. I think we can get it back if we can only get away. So come hell or high water, or your sister Shera, we leave on Monday. Okay?"

"Don't talk against my sister. Let's just leave. And let's paint ourselves out of this place. This is our jungle. I don't want anybody else in it."

So we got out the old white paint bucket and we painted out the wall. The trees disappeared and the wildflowers and then the birds and then the tiger's body, and then the smile on the face of the tiger. It was a bare wall again. We took down the paper fish and folded it. All that was left was us and the skylight. "In half a week we'll be lying under other stars," said Jason.

I wished he hadn't said it so loud. You know how the gods are, so jealous.

I wasn't sleeping well. Images moved through the dense seaweed and my head roared with the tide. I thought I heard the phone ring. It was dark and the dream dragged me back. Then the light came on. Jason was dressed. "What's the matter? It's still night."

"Better get up," he said. "I'm fixing coffee."

"What for?" I said. "What's wrong?"

He came to sit beside me. He made me sip from the hot cup. "Just take it easy. Will you promise to take it easy?"

"It's Shera! She took the pills again."

"This is worse than one of Shera's fake little suicides. Now I want you to listen to me first."

"What *hap*pened!"

"What happened has been happening from day one. From that first time in the hospital. Well it's going to keep on happening until she decides to make it not happen. Now it's not your concern any longer. You promise me that."

"Just *tell* me then!"

"Promise."

"I promise! *What!*"

"The jock, the guitar player. He got drunk and beat up on her."

"My God, the *baby!*"

"He had the brains to wheel the baby outside. But some joker took the carriage down the beach and a couple of drunks found the carriage and had it for hours before the cops found it. The baby's okay but he's been taken into protective custody. They filed charges against Shera. I guess this time she won't get it back so easy."

"She must have tried to kick him out. He must have got sore at her. It's my *fault*, Jason!"

"Will you stop it, *please!*"

"But *I* told her to get rid of him!"

It wasn't Shera. It wasn't my sister. It was someone with blackened eyes almost swollen shut. Her lips were so bruised she could hardly move them when she spoke. She held my hands while she tried to talk to me. "I was getting rid of him, just like you said. I never meant to be serious with him. I was just letting him hang around on account of Brian. I think he was crazy or something. I tried to do it the way you said but he hit me."

I couldn't look at her. *God help me not to look at her.*

"I begged him not to hurt my baby. Did he hurt my baby?"

"The baby is okay. Don't worry about the baby."

She lay back on the pillow, relieved. "If you see Brian now," she said, "tell him he can come back home." They must have given her a sedative. She seemed to be drifting into a drugged sleep. She brought her hands up slowly to her damaged face. "Have I been punished enough now?"

Momma and Mrs. Casamira stood in the hospital corridor. Momma was so stricken I hardly recognized her. She and Mrs. Casamira watched me with cat's eyes, following me as I walked down the hall. Jason moved me out of sight. He found me a place to sit and brought me coffee.

"I did it," I said. "I told her to get rid of him."

"Damn right," he said. "She needed to get rid of him. He could have killed her or the baby. So you did what was right. It was her own fault for fooling around with the guy. She was warned."

"It was my *fault*, Jason."

He pulled up a chair in front of me and made me look at him. "I sat in this hospital corridor once before with you, and then I got up and walked away. I'm not walking away this time. This time I walk you out of this mess. Do you understand me, Molly?"

"I don't understand anything," I said numbly. "What happened to my old nostalgia, my little family on the prairie, my sweet funny mother and her antics and my crazy kid sister and her dumb pranks? When did my little family comedy turn into a tragedy?"

"It always was," he said. "I told you that from the beginning."

I sat in my little window seat, but the whole place was empty now. The books were in boxes. The kitchen things, all except what we were taking in our packs, were wrapped in cartons. Jason was starting to organize the backpacks. He tied up my typewriter case so that I could carry it with me. I couldn't even move to help him. I tried to think about something but no thoughts came. "You shouldn't have taken down the fish yet," I said. "It's too bleak in here."

"Just three more days," he said. "Just put yourself into suspended animation. Take a time trip or something."

"How can I leave her in this mess?" I said.

"It's her mess," he said. "It's not your mess anymore. You can't help her. So just let go now."

She sat on the edge of the hospital bed gingerly washing her face from a pan of soapy water, testing the edges of her wounded and battered eyes with the tips of her fingers. The swelling was beginning to go down. At least I could recognize her. "Are you feeling any better?"

"What do you think?" she said. "Are you taking me home or what? They said I could go home this morning."

"I think Momma wants to take you home, Shera. She's bringing the car. Jason and I don't have a car anymore."

"How can Momma come if she's taking care of the baby?"

I watched her press the warm cloth to her face and wince. "Didn't Momma tell you?"

She took the cloth away. "Tell me what?"

"They picked up the baby again. He's back in the shelter. You have to go to a hearing tomorrow to get him out. I thought she told you."

She overturned the washbasin. She got so hysterical I had to ring for the nurse. *"Why did they take my baby! I didn't do anything except what you told me! I do what everybody tells me and look what happens to me! Get me my baby back!"*

I was furious with Momma. "Why did you let me go there with her thinking the baby was home all this time! Why didn't you tell me!"

I couldn't say anything else. There was no use. She looked so awful I hardly knew her. She looked half dead herself. "I want her room back the way it was," Momma said. "I want this house fixed up with flowers and when she walks in here I want the baby in her arms. Go get the baby, Molly."

"How am I going to get the baby?"

"Don't ask me," said Momma. "You're the one giving her all this advice. Be independent. Live on your own. Well this time she almost got killed. I want her home and I want her world the way it was and I want the baby back in this house. You go figure it out. You're the brilliant one. I'm just her mother."

Chapter Seven

❧

"PLEASE TALK to me," I said to Jason.

"Sure. What do you want to talk about? Byzantium? I'm ready for Byzantium. I'm ready for Spokane, Washington, or Chico, California, or Little Rock, Arkansas. I just want to get out of here. Okay?"

"How can you be so unfeeling?"

"I'm very feeling," he said. "If I told you what I felt right now you'd never believe it. But when it comes to your sister, I'm an insensitive sonofa-bitch."

"All I'm asking," I said, "is that we postpone the trip for a couple of weeks, just until she's out of the woods."

"When will she be out of the woods?" said Jason. "She lives in woods, she feeds in woods, she thrives in woods."

"You don't understand! She only missed the hearing

because she was afraid to go with her face that way! It's just postponed until Tuesday."

"Good. She'll get the baby back on Tuesday and she can move in with your mother on Tuesday. That's where she'll end up anyhow. That's the way she wants it and that's the way your mother wants it. So you'll invest a couple of bucks in a transatlantic call and you'll find out on Tuesday."

"But she can't go to court without me. She's scared to death."

"She won't go, you mean. She's done this over and over again. You're a slow learner when it comes to Shera."

"But it was different this time. She had a work training program lined up and she was joining a therapy group. What if they take the baby away from her because of me?"

"What is so special about your sister," said Jason, "that she can bust up people's lives and everybody else feels responsible? She's done every damn thing she's ever wanted! She didn't want to study so she didn't study. She wanted to screw around, so she screwed around. She wanted a husband, she wanted a baby. So she got them. While everybody felt rotten and guilty around her. What about Brian, that poor bastard? What about the baby? It almost got hurt once, it almost got hurt twice. Does that baby have to get itself killed before somebody lowers the boom on your sister? And all you do is make excuses for her!"

"But she's never had an easy time! Never! She's always taken lumps!"

"Well it's her life and her lumps, Molly. Let her go to court and get her own baby. Let her show them she can take care of it."

"Just a week, until it's settled then!"

"No," he said.

"Can't you give an inch? I'm in agony over this."

"I know you are," he said. "And there's nothing I can do about this agony. But I sure am going to save you from the next agony. We're leaving Monday. Period."

The whole house was in mourning. Momma kept herself locked in her room. The shades were drawn. Shera lay on the sofa under a blanket as if she were cold. "It wasn't my fault I got beat up," she said. "Why are they keeping my baby?"

"Nobody is keeping your baby. Monday you start the therapy. That afternoon you start the work training. You go into court on Tuesday and show them that it's all okay. Then take the baby back to Momma's until the apartment comes through. It's only a few days. I'll call you from England on Tuesday."

"I can't *go* alone! And I can't take Momma. You know how Momma gets. They'll ask me questions and I'll get upset and cry and they'll take my baby away for good. Please if you love me, go with me. We swore a blood oath, and now you're running out on me. *Please* Molly, you don't know what it is to have a baby in your arms and have somebody take him away."

"You can do it," I said. "I can't."

" 'Won't' you mean," she said bitterly. "You got what you want so you don't care how I suffer. If anything awful happened to you, I'd never leave you."

As I closed the door, I heard her crying.

Jason laid out all the clothes to finish the backpacks. And he heated up TV dinners because all the dishes were gone. "Eat," he said. "I spent hours over a hot stove fixing dinner and you're not eating."

"Please don't do this to me," I begged.

"Nobody's doing anything to you. You're doing it to yourself."

"But you never wanted to go to Europe anyhow, so what difference does one summer vacation make?"

"It has nothing to do with Europe and you know it," said Jason. "It's bigger than a trip to Europe. Let go, Molly. We leave on Monday. So just let go."

"This is what I found in her bedroom," said Momma. She took a razor blade out of her pocket. "You're killing your sister."

"Nobody is killing her. All she has to do is prove she can take care of the baby. Why is she making this big thing out of it?"

"What is she," said Momma, "a criminal that she has to plead for her baby? What has she done but be hurt by men in her innocence. You swore a blood oath, Molly."

"There never was a blood oath," I said.

"Blood was spilled between you. More than once. And always it was her blood. Let your smartness be for something. That's why God made you smarter and her weaker. For a reason. For you to help her in time of need. She won't go to court without you. Do this one thing and go off happy. Go off and forget us. But don't take this one thing from your sister."

I tried one last time to reason with her. The room was swamped in gloom. Her face was almost back to normal, but marked with the loss of the baby. "I can't stop thinking about him," she said. "I can hear him screaming for me."

I tried to take her hand but she pulled it away. She writhed in pain. "They'll never give him to me. I do everything dumb, don't I. I have all my life. With school, with the boys, with Brian, and now with my baby. I want you to go now. I want you to have a really super time in Europe. I love you and I always have, Molly. So kiss me good-bye."

"Don't talk like this. By Tuesday you'll have him back and you'll feel like a fool for saying all this."

"We only were the two of us," she said. "Let one of us be happy at least." She reached up and kissed me good-bye. Then she turned her head to the wall. "You won't see me again," she said.

Chapter Eight

❧

IT WAS THE end of something. I just wasn't sure what. With the fish gone, the naked light made sharp shadow edges and poked mercilessly into the empty spaces.

We sat together on the mattress under the skylight that had been boarded up. Just an old ceiling now with the cobwebs showing.

"The first time you came up those stairs," said Jason, "you burst into this place like a firecracker."

"I guess I'm going out like a damp punk," I said. "Do you remember me the way I was? I seem to have lost something in the translation."

"Nothing's lost," he said. "You're in hibernation. You're all worn out."

"My head hurts so bad."

"Wait until we clear the dust of this place off our heels. We'll go to Delphi. We'll ask the Oracle what to do for headaches."

"I'll bet you wished a hundred times you could just dump me and run."

"Not a hundred times," he said.

"But you did sometimes, though."

"So what if I did? You've been reading me all these poems about how love is pain. So this is the pain. I said I was willing to wait it out."

It was all such a confusion. "I know I wanted so many things in my life. Now I can't remember what it was I wanted."

"I remember," he said. "You'll remember as soon as you let go." He made a warm place for me against his chest.

I held on to him. I knew I would drown if I didn't. "I want to let go of her but if I leave her, I'll see her in my nightmares for the rest of my life."

"We'll talk about it," he said, "while we're walking down the little back alleys of Soho."

We couldn't sleep. So he took out his recorder and sat, like Pan, playing me songs. Not exactly perfect but sweet and haunting. Then he gave me shelter in his arms. Then he reminded me of some stars I had forgotten, and dreams I had forgotten, and he took me time-tripping. We bent over tide pools I remembered and watched a certain cyprus tree out on the coast that bends back on itself and then stretches seaward, sort of looking toward the horizon. And then he sighed against my cheek and we huddled like puppies in the blankets. Sleep came softly on us. The last thing I remembered was Elizabeth Barrett Browning saying, *Haven't I taught you to recognize love? Well this is it, dummy.*

We were jolted by the knocking at the door downstairs. "Molly? Are you in there?"

It was Momma.

We almost killed ourselves getting dressed. And we were dizzy from going to sleep and coming back. And the light from the naked bulb swung from side to side because Jason had knocked against it in his haste. Momma still pounded on the door. "Can you hear me in there?"

I helped her up the ladder. The bulb made terrible shadows on our empty walls. All she could see was the barren room, and the bed, and Jason. Fury crossed her face when she looked at him. "So this is where you've been keeping my daughter."

"It wasn't like this . . ." I started to explain. What was the use. "Did you come to say good-bye to me, Momma?"

"I didn't come to say good-bye. I tried to phone you, but the phone was turned off. I came because Shera took the pills again."

Jason put an arm around me. "Don't believe it. Your sister is famous for pills."

If she had had a knife in her hand she would have stabbed him. She looked like death. "This morning. It happened this morning. They took her to the hospital and pumped her out."

"Where did she get the pills?" asked Jason. "If she was at home, where did she find pills?"

Momma forced herself to ignore him. "She's a sick girl, Molly. I don't know what will happen to her anymore." Momma started to cry but she forced back the tears. She pressed her handkerchief against her eyes. "She asked to see you before she went. Just come to see her before you run away from us."

I tried to move toward her but Jason held on to me. "What is it you expect from Molly? Does she have to keep bailing her sister out all her life?"

Momma turned on Jason with eyes that would cut ice. "Who are you to tell her what she can do or can't do or has to do? You've held her in this terrible place for your own selfish reasons. I know men like you. I know all the men like you. Some people have responsibilities closer to the heart. They know what family means."

"Let her go," said Jason. "If you love Molly, then let her go."

"Nobody is keeping her," said Momma. "She has a whole life in front of her, if this is the life she wants. But Shera has no life. Let Shera have something too. Let her have the baby."

The room buzzed around me. In the silence I could hear my sister crying and her baby crying. "I'll just go home for an hour," I said to Jason. "Just for an hour. Just give me an hour, *please?*" He tried to hold me but I separated myself. "You asked me to trust you, now trust me. I swear to you I'll be back in an hour."

He let me go. He released me. He lay down on the mattress and covered his eyes with his arm. "I'll wait an hour," he said.

"This is the man you're throwing your life away for?" said Momma. "He'll give you an hour of his precious time when your world is falling apart. He can't spare you more than an hour."

"Just stop it," I said. "All I'm doing is coming home to see my sister, so just cut it out."

I bent to kiss Jason good-bye. "An hour," I said.

He didn't answer me.

Momma started to say something in the car. "Don't talk to me," I said. "Just don't say anything."

"At least he hasn't turned your heart to stone," she said.

The room smelled sick and medicinal. I didn't let Momma come in. I turned on the lamp. Shera stirred, but she didn't speak. I sat on the side of the bed and shook her. She turned over and looked toward me, but her eyes weren't alive. Then she realized I was there. "You've come. Momma said you would but I didn't believe it."

I made her sit up. I brushed out her hair and brought her a hot washcloth for her face and I went into the kitchen and got bread and butter and jam. As if nothing had happened and it was the old days. Momma came to the door with a dish of cake. "Just keep out of it," I said to her. Mrs. Casamira stood behind Momma with the coffeepot. "We're not insulted," she said. "You'll be rewarded in heaven for helping your sister."

Shera and I just pushed time away and went back to the old days. We stuffed ourselves with jam sandwiches and drank chocolate milk the way we did on hot sticky summer days and then we tried to remember little things out of our lost past, dumb incidents, things that were silly, old programs we watched. Then she threw her arms around my neck and cried. When she was finished, she dried her eyes on the sheet.

"Are you better now?"

"Now that you're here. I wanted you so much. It doesn't seem real when you're not here."

"Let's just look at facts then. Who ever said they wanted to keep your baby?"

"Nobody."

"Then why do you think they will?"

"Momma says they try to keep babies. They take them and people pay money to adopt them."

"That's what I thought. Well Momma's a liar. You're going to get the baby back. You're going to stop doing things to hurt yourself and get back your own baby."

"When you sit here and say do it, I think I can. But when you're gone, it's terrible. Please stay and help me. I don't mean for a long time, just for a little while. Jason can wait just a little while! When I'm here Momma puts me to bed and she stuffs me with things and I think I'll just die here. Let's get a place of our own, just the two of us. You don't know how bad I am with social workers and court people. Just like school. They ask me questions and even if I know the answer, I freeze up. Just help me this one last time. Then when I'm settled in the place and the baby is with me, I want you to go. Anyplace in the world. Do all the wonderful things. Do this one thing for me, Molly, and I'll never forget you all my life!"

Her eyes came to life again. We both curled in her bed sucking candy. That old bed with the dog-eared books and the calico dolls and all the years of the two of us together. "Do you think you could make it this time?"

"It's all been so awful," she said. "I was so dumb about Brian. Maybe he'll hear if I get myself a job and all. Maybe he'll come back if I change."

"I wish you could tell that to Jason."

"If Jason really loved you, he'd wait awhile. I don't believe in love anymore. But I believe in being sisters. And I'll do everything you say. I'll be in that therapy at nine o'clock in the morning. And then I'll take a bus downtown and I'll see about the work thing and the nursery for the baby. And then we'll find our own place and start again. Momma made us weird. You said so yourself. And we have to work our way out of it. An hour ago I wanted to be dead. Now you're here. Maybe our luck will change. Maybe the cards will be different now."

My hour was up. I called a cab to drive me back. If I missed my magic hour, the studio would be changed into a pumpkin and Jason would be gone. I prayed all the way. I said all the magic numbers and made vows to Zeus and to Loki and to Momma's God.

But everything was there. A little light glowed in the dormer window. Jason was still there! I ran up the stairs. He lay on the mattress, just as I had left him. He must have fallen asleep. "Jason?"

"I'm not sleeping," he said.

I covered him with a million kisses. I took our little cooking pot out of the backpack and boiled us some water for tea with one old teabag I found. We let the bitter tea warm us. Eye to eye. Jason's eyes. He leaned over and kissed my face. I kissed his mouth. "Dear heart," I said, "how do I love thee, let me name the ways."

"That seems like a million years ago," he said.

"It's not. I'm back again. I worked it all out in my head now. My head is clear again. I can see stars."

"Can you?" he said.

"I was good for you. You were good for me. It was perfect for us before and it will be again. We just rushed things too much. This is how we'll do it. You leave for Europe tomorrow. You go to all the galleries. You soak up the art. You stay there for four weeks."

He put down the teacup.

"*Listen* to me. Just four weeks while I get Shera settled on her own. Everything has changed for her, Jason. She's really been burned this time. She's not the person she was. She just wants to get away from Momma's house and make it on her own. The way I do. She starts therapy in the morning and a work program in the afternoon. Tuesday we get the baby and we find an apartment and I stay with her, just for a month. She is my sister. I have to do that for her, don't I? After four weeks Momma is taking money out of her savings to buy a commercial flight. She'll send me off with her blessing."

"Four weeks," he said emptily.

"Please don't say it that way." I stroked his face, his dear face, his sweet face. But he moved my hand away and wouldn't let me touch him. "It's just four weeks out of a life. I'll take TWA or something and I'll meet you. Whither thou wantest. Under the Arc de Triomphe. Near Big Ben. No. At the Acropolis. I'll meet you at high noon, we'll synchronize our watches, Greek time. You'll be standing there, near the temple of Hera, and I'll come flying toward you across the stones . . ."

He stood up and walked to the window. "You're still a little dreamer, a little fancier. You live in bits and patches of fantasy."

"It's not a fantasy. Then I can do what I need to do for my sister and be with you too. And when it's all over and we know we've sacrificed and done our best, we can go away. And then we can talk about what's happened, and find Byzantium, and the stars."

"You're really no different from your sister, are you," he said.

Pig's bladder across the head. "What did you say?"

He turned around and said it to my face. "You're no different from your sister."

I withdrew into a little cocooned place and sheltered myself. "I don't want to hear this."

"You're very selective in your hearing," he said. "She wanted to get away from your mother so she latched on to Brian, but when she had to make it with him on the outside, she couldn't do it. So she dumped him. Isn't that what you're doing with me?"

"But that's not true! If it weren't for Shera I'd be going!"

"Why is it Shera who decides how you live and what you do? No matter how hard you pull away, you're still back with Shera on step one."

"But it's different with her this time! I swear!"

"You're even beginning to sound like her."

"Why didn't you come with me to see her then? Why didn't you meet with her face to face and see the mess she's in? And it's not just Momma's fault, it's partly my fault. All she needs is this one last boost up."

"Don't you understand the givens by now? If you go back to her this time, you'll always go back to her. I know that. Why don't you know that?"

"It's not true! You only see your side of things, you never see mine. You want to pin me down because *you* want me where you can understand me. Well my heart needs to be free sometimes."

"Free of me, you mean. That's the crux of it, isn't it? You never meant to go off with me any more than she meant to go off with Brian. I guess I knew that from the beginning."

"That's not true! Don't mix me up when I've figured it out at last. It's only four weeks. Four weeks out of a lifetime and I'll be free of everything. Then we can work it all out. Why can't you just wait those four crummy weeks and find out who was right?"

"Let go of Shera or let go of me," he said.

The earth was just a little off its axis. "Hey," I said, "I'm not holding you." I didn't say that, my mouth said it. "It's just like that last time, isn't it? Things get messy with Shera and you just run out. Is that what you want this time? Another good-bye and good luck?"

"Is that what you want from me?" he said. "Little flip witticisms like the last time? You've got my heart on the table and my gut on the floor. What are you going to do, make little literary jokes while I'm bleeding to death, Molly? I said let *go* of her or let go of me!"

"Don't *do* this to me! You know I can't just let her drown!"

He put on his jacket and his shoes. He picked up his pack and settled it on his back. I didn't believe what he was doing. He was just trying to scare me. Then I heard his steps descending the stairs. I ran to the top of the ladder. But he was already on the street. I ran to the little window but he had already walked out of sight. I listened for his steps, but all I heard were echoes. "Four lousy weeks!" I screamed out of the window.

I sat alone for about an hour, in the empty room, with all the ghosts. For a while I heard snatches of our old conversations, like echoes, that lingered. I saw scenes moving before me like shadows, and I heard Jason's laughter and my laughter. And then the laughter faded and died. Other voices came. Loki, and bits of more subtle laughter, and squeaks and moans and closing doors and wind in the cracks. Silence followed. And then I heard my heart beating and the shadows frightened me.

I left the light burning. I took my coat and hefted my pack and climbed unsteadily down the steps. I

walked away. The pack was too heavy. I could hardly
lift it. I stopped at a phone booth and called Momma.
She came to pick me up. She stuffed my things into
the trunk of the car. She hugged me and kissed me.
Then she settled me in and locked the car so murderers
couldn't jump in and assault us. And we went home.

I stood in Momma's living room again, with her little
plastic-covered sofa and prints of the English country-
side and all the ivy that waved little green tendrils at
me. "She's asleep," said Momma. "When she knew you
hadn't run off and deserted her, she gave a great sigh
as if all the poisons of her body left her, and she fell
asleep. Tomorrow she starts a new life. And the worst
is over for you too, Molly. I know how this hurts now.
But the worst is past. And someday you'll look back
and you'll know what you did for your family. Your
golden life is still ahead. Wait and see."

I was numb. I didn't seem to have much volition.
She turned down my bed. She laid out the night-
clothes that she had kept clean and folded in my drawer. I lay down on my old bed and sank like a rock.

Chapter Nine

❁

A LITTLE light filtered down through the dim water. I lay at the bottom swishing my fins in that half-light. Jason swam by. The water rippled softly. *I'm not gone. I'm still back at the studio, hurry home. We'll make a pot of espresso and I'll lie with my head on your lap and you'll read me sonnets* . . .

The door to the bedroom inched open. Momma peeked in, Mrs. Casamira behind her. "She's up finally." Momma carried in a bed tray, a mess of food and a vase with a rose in it. The smell of bacon and doughnuts. My stomach turned. "We'll fatten you up," said Momma. "This time you'll have a proper meal for once."

"A gem," said Mrs. Casamira. "A gem among gems."

I think I wasn't focusing too clearly. I thought I heard the sound of an airplane motor overhead, dron-

139

ing above me, and then it floated out of hearing. "What time is it?"

"Almost noon. You were that tired. I don't think you had a decent night's sleep in months."

I listened again for the plane. All I heard was my heart, beating without any kind of rhythm. Just a sort of plop, plop, like water dripping at night from a faucet in an empty studio in an old grocery warehouse.

"It will be like a bad dream," said Momma. "It will pass. We'll all look back on it, you'll see. Tomorrow the baby will be home again. And wait until you hear the news Mrs. Casamira has brought us."

"Later," I said. "Let me sleep, okay?"

"You'll have plenty of time to sleep," said Momma. "You're home again."

They stood waiting until I put on my robe. My heart tried feebly to say *Jason* or something, but I think it was badly bleeding. Or else it had been surgically removed and there was a big hole where it used to be. I tried to picture Shera happy again and the baby happy, and my four weeks finished, and there I was running across the hallowed ancient stones of the Acropolis, Hera smiling down on me, Poseidon, his trident raised, smiling down on me, Molly favored of the gods. And there, on the steps of the Parthenon, Jason waited. I waved to him. I ran toward him, my hair flying behind me, in the sweet clarity of the Athens light . . .

"Hurry," said Momma.

She had filled the house with flowers. Flowers in every pot and every pitcher, on the tables, in every corner. Some of them were roses cut from Mrs. Casamira's garden, heavy-scented roses so that the room smelled like a mortuary.

They pulled me over to the dining room table. My will to protest also had been surgically removed. "Listen to this," said Momma. "You know Mrs. Casamira's house, that big old place with nobody in it since she's been alone?"

"I have rooms and rooms in that place," said Mrs. Casamira. "I'm rattling around."

"So why should you and your sister struggle to pay rent for some strange apartment? You can have the whole top floor of her house, right close by."

"It would be like your own place," said Mrs. Casamira. "You wouldn't even know that I was around." She shuffled her deck of cards and cut them. She held up an ace. "Ace of diamonds. Gems returned. It will all be aces now, you'll see."

"I'll talk it over with Shera," I said, "but I don't think she'll go for it. Thanks anyhow, but no thanks."

"You'll see," said Momma. "You'll think about it. You'll talk it over with your sister."

Shera pushed through the door stretching and yawning. "What will she talk over with me?"

I had the feeling that the elevator cable broke suddenly and I dropped about fifty floors. "What is she *doing* here!"

"Where should she be?" asked Momma.

"In the therapy! This morning! And she had a twelve o'clock appointment downtown!"

"Oh God!" said Shera. "What *time* is it! She promised to wake me up at seven!"

"How could I wake her?" said Momma. "Her first night's sleep in a month. Anyhow this is the best therapy she could have, a family that loves her."

"Why did you need *her* to wake you up!" I cried. "You have your own alarm clock! Why didn't you set the alarm!"

"She said *she* would do it, that's why!"

"What do you want from the child?" said Momma. "Look at her. Ask her how she feels after all she's been through."

"I ache in every bone," said Shera. "I'm so tired and all."

"You can still make it to your downtown appointment," I said. "Go get dressed. I'll phone them we've been delayed. I'll drive you down myself."

"This child hasn't eaten in two weeks," said Momma. "I'm not going to have her sick with mono and the baby on my hands to boot. Give her a day to rest up. Tomorrow we'll all go and bring the baby home."

Shera looked to me helplessly. Momma pushed a plate of cake under her nose. Mrs. Casamira ran to the kitchen for the coffee. "This is the happiest day of my life," said Momma. "My girls are home again. This one is still beautiful in spite of everything, and this one is still brilliant and now that she's come through the shoals, she'll use her brilliance as God intended."

It was funny the way it happened. The whole picture stopped. They sat there frozen in time. Mrs. Casamira pouring coffee into Shera's cup, her stinky cigarette clamped between her teeth, Momma leaning over Shera, smiling and fussing with Shera's hair, and Shera like a caged bird between them. They lost color. Like an old faded tintype.

I guess I just stepped out of it.

I went into the bedroom and took off my robe. I thought about Cleopatra putting hers on. I guess I had *mortal* longings in me. I wondered whatever gave me such a yen to live. I put on the clothes I had taken off the night before. I lifted the pack. He must have put rocks in it, it was so heavy. *He.* Meaning Jason. My chest tightened, either in pain or love or anger. I wasn't able to tell the difference much at the moment.

I came back into the living room. They were there, my sister and my mother, and Mrs. Casamira of the cards. Still arguing, still fussing. The way they had forever. Only it was different for me. The air was different. Lighter maybe. Or else my head had cleared.

Momma saw me first. "What are you doing!"

It was my sister I looked to. She was the one who worried me. "Leaving I guess. I never should have come back."

"But it's not my fault!" Shera protested. "I wanted to go this morning! I'll go tomorrow! I swear!"

What I would never know, and what I needed to know, was if all the things I told her to do came out of love. I think I loved her. It hurt me to look at her the way she was, still bluish under the eyes. "It's better for both of us if I go," I said. "I think it's better for you."

"Don't *be* like this," Shera begged. "You don't know what I've been through."

"I do know," I said. "And unless you make it stop now, it's going to happen a million times more. I know that for sure."

"What about my baby!" she said. "You'll make me lose my baby."

I thought about it carefully before I answered her. "I think if you really wanted him you would have gone a couple of days ago, by yourself, and you would have said it's *my* baby, and *I* can take care of him, and *I* want to."

"You don't think I want my baby?" she cried. "Liar!"

"This is your advice?" said Momma. "Is this what you tell to a weak sixteen-year-old girl, with all your wisdom?"

"I don't think she's been all that weak," I said. "She's been strong enough to get what she wanted until now. Why is she making such a soap opera out of this? She could have lived happily out there on the beach with Brian and the baby. She could have had the fun of going off to a new place with somebody who loved her. If that's what she really wanted. She could have been in clover. Instead of hysterical and making everybody do her thing for her. I don't understand why."

"Don't be a schoolgirl fool," said Momma. "You don't understand about life."

"Where is there life in this house? She's always dying about something and you're always dying about something. The only thing alive around here is the ivy."

"You promised!" Shera pleaded. "You swore! Make her!" she appealed to Momma. "She's just being mean because she wants what *she* wants. She always gets what *she* wants."

"Jesus Mary, Shera, you get what you want too! Not what Momma wants! She wants you mummified in a box where there isn't any love! This is a nunnery, and I don't even think God knows it's here."

"To me you'd say this?" said Momma. "Who has suffered agonies with two foolish daughters who should still be schoolgirls with report cards and dates? Not suffering the way I have all my life?"

"Who told you to suffer?" I said. "Because my father ran out and her father ran out? I don't even think they ran out. I think you kicked them out. Maybe if anybody had believed in love around here, Shera and I wouldn't have had to run either."

Momma fell back, wounded to the core.

"I'm not *blaming* you," I said. I tried to stroke her hands, to comfort her. "You're just as stuck as we are. I know that! Maybe worse. You were so scared of everything, you walled yourself up in this little alcove and you pulled us in with you. But we want out, Momma. It's your wall. All you have to do is take it down."

Mrs. Casamira shoved coffee at us. She sliced cake. "Don't say these things to your mother. It's a sin. You'll regret it all your life."

"What life? I just happen to think my sister can make it. I guess I'm the only one who does."

"She can't go off and leave me," wept Shera. "She'll be sorry. When she comes back I'll be dead."

"You're dead now," I said. "Help her live," I said to Momma. "Help us both. Tell my sister that if she really wants to keep this baby she has to be strong and pull her life together. And tell me to leave now and find my own place. Send me away and I swear I'll love you all my life. And if you really need me, I'll come, even from Istanbul." I saw Momma turn pale. "Just for once see us separate. She's Shera. I'm Molly."

Momma looked to Shera who was crying with her head on the table, and to the sorceress of the stinky cigarettes who sat flipping through the tarot looking for answers. "Don't ask me this thing," begged Momma. "Have compassion. Don't ask me to choose."

I put my eyes on them one more time to set them in memory.

Then I walked out.

I didn't look back. I would have turned to stone.

Chapter Ten

❦

ONE DAY! He could have waited one lousy day and the world would have been right. That close to happiness, and he ran. But there were still ties between us. If not love, then money. His money and my money, a hundred strands of the web of our life together, my stuff in his pack and his stuff in mine.

I tried the studio first. I dragged the eight blocks from the bus with that monster backpack on my back. My heart was still sick from Shera, and every staggering step said that *this* was the freedom he wanted me to have in Europe. I mean bitter. "Jason!" I called. Two faces looked down from my dormer window, a guy with a beard and a sort of apprehensive girl with a long braid over her shoulder. "He was here looking for you!" called the guy. "I'm *sorry!*" called the girl.

What was *she* sorry for? Herself probably. She was just moving in, and here she saw the end of it.

I had to take the pack off. I hauled it by the straps to

the phone booth and called Richard Cotter. "What the hell is happening with you and Jason?" he said.

"Where is he now?"

"At the Greyhound station."

Greyhound. So I dragged myself back to the bus and headed for the Greyhound station and Jason. My morning and my evening star. Eclipse.

The Greyhound station was jammed with people coming or going. And us. Jason and me, in limbo. He was lying on a bench, one leg hanging over the side and his head on his backpack. I dumped my stuff near the bench. He saw me. He sat up. I felt gall burning my throat. He watched me, saying nothing. Well he had said enough last night, hadn't he.

Only his eyes took the edge off my anger, those old Hamlet melancholy eyes, the sad eyes I hadn't seen since those first days. Hadn't those eyes been alive with me? *So I wasn't using you! That was a lie! I'm not Shera! I gave as much as I got! I loved you!*

Liar.

The voice in my head said it.

It wasn't a lie! He was happy with me! Always! I made him happy!

Bad enough to lie to yourself. You had the nerve to tell the truth to Shera and Momma, didn't you. Why can't you tell the truth to him.

So what was truth then? He always knew the truth. I was a small mushy snail looking for a shell. I wanted a fixed star, for a while anyhow. I disarranged his life, I moved every piece of his life around to suit myself. And I never would have gone to Kansas. Jesus Mary, I never would have got married. I would have found my way out.

"You okay?" he said.

The *last* thing in the world I wanted was a kind remark! The cutting edge of my anger returned."Did you care, *really?* You *bet* I'm okay! If you'd waited one rotten day you'd have *seen* I was okay!"

I said it with caustic, bone-cutting, nerve-searing

acid. I saw him wince, I saw his eyes glaze over, he turned away.

Truth is terrible. You can drown in truth. Oh God, I loved him, the same way he loved me last night when he walked out. I put my arms around him from the back and held the front of him. I laid my face against his back. *"Jason . . ."*

After a while he held my hands against his chest. And then he turned around and dried at the edges of his eyes with his fingers. I kissed his eyes about a dozen times. Let them watch if they wanted. This was a bus station. You were supposed to.

All the games were over. We looked at each other and got teary again and had to wait again.

Finally I said, "What did you put in the pack to weigh it down like that?"

"The cooking stuff," he said, "and I think I accidentally put in a couple of my books."

"You never really wanted to go to Europe."

"I would have gone," he said. "You never wanted to go to Kansas."

I started to say, *I would have gone.* Truth was the light on the water. "I never would have gone. I would have figured a way out of it."

The truth was scaring us both. We fell together like two drowning souls adrift on the last floating spar. "Well why were you going to Kansas anyway," I said. "Only to get me away from Momma. Look. I'm away. So what do you want to do now?"

He pushed back my hair and kissed the side of my face. "I am so damn tired of all this," he said. "I only wanted a nice quiet uncomplicated working summer in Mendocino."

"And you got an albatross instead." I took a terrible deep breath before I said my next words. "Jesus Mary, go take it. Go find out about the painting once and for all."

"Come with me," he said. "You'll work and I'll work and we'll walk along the beach and talk about it."

Truth hit me like waves. Knocked the air out of me. I put his Michelangelic hand to my cheek. I kissed his hand. "If I ran back to you now, I'd never know if that was why I left *her*. I loved her too, and I left her. And I'd never know if I came to you because I ran scared again. Do you understand what I mean?"

I sensed the edge of bitterness. "So what are you going to do, go up to a mountain someplace and do penance for your sister?"

"I only know I have to work it out alone."

"Alone? It's terrible alone," he said. "I know alone."

I wanted to hold him the same way he wanted to hold me. But we sat apart. "Then paint *alone*. Paint *terrible*. Then you'll know."

He took the tickets out of his pocket and handed me mine. "Somebody bought the standby so you can cash it in." He gave me my book of traveler's checks, the ones I'd signed. "It's not even. You want all the numbers or what?"

I was scared. "I don't want to separate from you!"

"Then what is it you want?" he asked softly.

"I want to go away alone and think it all out," I said. "I want to move into a world that flows with light and energy. I want to see color, and oddness, and danger, and fun. I want to write poems and survive. How do I know?"

"Byzantium," he said wryly. "You make Byzantium out of cotton candy."

"Then that's what I do," I said.

"You'll trade the ticket in for another flight. You'll end up in a crummy hotel without a john, you'll get lost or cheated or taken advantage of. You'll get in trouble, you'll be scared to death."

"I'll be scared," I said, "but not to death."

He looked into my face. "Tell me the truth for once. Do you love me?"

"The truth," I said, "as much as I know the truth is that I love you now, and I always loved you and I always will love you, as much as I know about love."

He kissed me with the sweetness of old kisses, which are unequaled in the natural world. "My luck to fall for a poet." Then he let me go. "I can't promise that I'll be around when you come back, Molly. I just don't know."

"I can't promise I'll be back," I said.

And in my head this voice warned me: *Careful. This is rare. It may not come your way again.*

And then a voice said: *Destiny is like a river.*

And then a voice said: *Love is a fixed point. When you're truly anchored in love, only then are you free. Love is the buoy.*

"We'll talk about it," I said.

I hefted my pack on my back and I walked away. Not looking back. I was aware that I still had his books and he had my poems and other stuff of mine. Okay. I mean I'd made enough gestures, now what was, was.

I caught the airport bus. I was nervous until we were out of range of the station, so that even if I turned around I couldn't see his face.

It was done then.

I was tired. I lay against the seat. The sun through the window was hot on me. I felt like a lizard on a rock.

So this is how it happens. You lie back and the bus bumps along and you drift and you dream. It all begins in fantasy, all the wonderful things, the way life ought to be, and the way people ought to love, and the joy, and the adventure, and the stories, and the pictures. Then you have to wake up and sweat and make it all come out.

In my fantasy I saw Shera, the baby hanging out of the little seat strapped to her back. *Molly!* she cried. *I'm so glad to see you! I decided I could make it with the baby! It's so hard, but I found this little nursery and I've got a part-time job and I go to Continuation and I've met this neat guy. The baby is so beautiful, Molly, I read to him every night. He's trying to make sounds already . . . did you know they start to talk that way?*

I drifted back to Momma and Mrs. Casamira. The two of them in night school taking pottery. Making these pots for Momma's cruddy ivy. Doing these great pots and talking to new people. Momma looked up from her sticky clay and smiled. *You look so happy, Molly. That's all I know and all I need to know.*

I would write little stories about it, like *I Remember Momma*, when my eyes didn't tear up and my throat didn't get so tight.

Anyhow, you couldn't avoid tears I guess. But in back of the tears you had images, like birds flying over water.

Anyhow, in general it was a fine day, a good hot day, and the streets, as we rolled along, were like rivers running wide in all directions. I lay back and dreamed. Of Crete, and Thessaloniki, and the marketplace in Fez, and of this woman in Istanbul, in a flowered pantaloon, leaning up against a tree and watching the sky. I drifted until the wheels of the bus left the ground and we drifted westerly toward the sea.

ABOUT THE AUTHOR

BLOSSOM ELFMAN is the author of two previous novels, *The Girls of Huntington House* and *A House for Jonnie O.*, which was an ALA Notable Book in 1977. She lives with her husband in Los Angeles, where she is at work on her next book.

A Special Preview of
the opening pages of the highly
acclaimed novel by the author of
A HOUSE FOR JONNIE O.

THE GIRLS OF
HUNTINGTON HOUSE
By
Blossom Elfman

"Has the juices of life in it . . . A rare treat."
—Bel Kaufman, author of
Up the Down Staircase

Bid the Boys Goodbye

If it weren't for Mr. Vanderveld's asthma I might never have come to Huntington House. I certainly never applied to teach there. I was solicited. And I accepted the assignment not so much with enthusiasm as out of desperation. Yet, when the semester ended and Doris asked me in that voice of hers, "I don't suppose you expect to return in the fall?" my intention was as clear as her implication. I will return, in spite of Doris, in spite of Downtown which is threatening either to dismiss me or transfer me because of what I said to their idiot graduation speaker. I doubt if they will do either. I'm not sure anyone else wants the job.

•

Huntington House is three stories of sooty gray stone and tired ivy, dusty windows that have to be opened outward by a hand crank, long dreary corridors of buckled linoleum, dark molding layered with varnish, cavernous bathrooms where the broken edges of little diamond tiles pinch the bare feet. The girls who live there are unmotivated, unreceptive, and critical. They are not eager to be taught and their primary verbal skill lies in the art of complaint.

"I *can't* do my paragraph. I don't *feel* well."

"Where don't you feel well, Orenthia? I'll ask Nurse Caulfield to send up some aspirins because I don't want you to miss the lesson on paragraphing."

"I'm not going to *write* any more paragraphs. I'm having false labor pains."

"How can you be having false labor pains? You're only in your fifth month."

"Well, I *said* false labor, didn't I!"

Huntington House is a maternity home. My students are under eighteen, unmarried, and pregnant. And I am tired of the joker who asks, "What can you teach pregnant teen-agers that they don't already know?"

I was hired to teach them English. I came to teach them Dylan Thomas and *Ethan Frome* and dependent clauses and punctuation and iambic pentameter. I wonder now if any of that is significant. There is too much that I cannot teach them, not yet, since there are things I don't understand myself, things concerned with the confusion of the heart. Not just theirs but mine. And although I came here by chance I will fight for this assignment, not only for what I can teach but because my own education is incomplete.

Before Mrs. Vanderveld made her sudden departure from Huntington House, I was in fact a member of the faculty of the most coveted school in the city, an architect's creation in glass and natural wood and stone, organically integrated into expensively verdant hills, and crammed with forty verbal adolescents to a class, five classes a day, and homeroom. Sometimes, with luck, thirty-five, but at least five of those were causing me anguish. Like Danny Ornstein, for instance, and his bare feet.

It doesn't make any difference to me if a student comes in with bare feet, but *bare feet* was the issue of the day. It was the mad bare-feet season and shoes were specifically required. I didn't make the rules. I only wanted to teach "The Love Song of J. Alfred Prufrock," and Danny Ornstein came slap-slapping into the room, maneuvering to catch my eye. I did not want a confrontation. I only wanted to teach *imagery and the sea.*

"Hot," he said as he stomped heavily in the vicinity of my desk. "I hate to be overdressed in hot weather."

"Where are you overdressed, Danny? If you sit down and stop weaving around you won't feel the heat."

"I admire you new teachers who wear flats. You don't need to stagger around on heels like some of the phonies in this place."

I kept my eyes on the class and away from his feet but I could smell them.

"I'd like to hit the imagery of 'Prufrock.' That we started yesterday as you remember? Four images, the sea, the hands, and what else?"

"Feet!" he called, sliding behind his desk and sticking his feet into the aisle.

"Where are there feet in 'Prufrock'?"

"Where he says 'Do I dare descend the stair with a bald spot in the middle of my hair.' "

"Where are the feet?"

"How could he descend the stair without feet?" He tattooed the floor with his heels.

"Danny," I said, "pick up your feet and get out. It's only eight-eighteen and it's already hot and I want to teach a lesson and you're being obstructionist. I'm not in the mood for social issues and I have four more classes and I'm tired of your feet. So please go soak your feet and your head in the men's room and let's get back to sea imagery!"

"Aha! So you have feelings! So you can be stirred to anger! Why don't you leave the sterile poetry of yesterday and throw yourself behind a valid cause. It's *tomorrow* that's important!"

"Feet? You want me to throw myself behind feet? And tomorrow I'm giving a test on the imagery of T. S. Eliot! So why does he make such an issue about water?"

"To wash Danny's feet!" yelled someone.

Unfortunately I didn't remember someone's name. It was the third week of the semester and I was facing almost two hundred students a day. And I was tired of it. It pressed in on me. I wanted to retire to where I could teach in a modicum of peace. To manageable numbers.

And I told as much to my friend J. over the phone that evening.

"I can't survive with these large classes. I have to get out."

"Again?" he asked.

"What do you mean 'again'? In that tone?"

"You've been teaching for three years and this is your third transfer. What are you running away from?"

"I'm not running. I'm searching for a comfortable space. I haven't found my dimension."

Let him make his insinuations.

"And if I am running, it's the 'madding crowd' I'm running from."

"Very literary," he said wryly. "But ask yourself—is it the truth?"

J. isn't Socrates. He doesn't teach school. I do.

And so when the time for transfer requests came around I desperately questioned my principal. Wasn't there a place where a teacher could teach to small groups, where a teacher could function in the way a teacher is supposed to function?

"If you have a little money in the bank start a small private school. Do you know that there are teachers who would give their eyeteeth to get this spot? If you want solitude, teach in a hospital. A nice quiet hospital room and a student in a body cast. Then you can teach one-to-one instead of one-to-forty. If you don't mind waiting for him to get out of surgery to deliver your lecture."

"One-to-one!" The thought intrigued me.

"I wasn't serious," he added. "You wouldn't like it."

"Why wouldn't I like it?"

"These are bedridden kids. I know you. You're better with bare feet than with twisted feet. It isn't your vocation."

Everyone thinks he knows my vocation. J. included.

"Look," I said, "all kids are handicapped these days. And all teachers." Sounds of slapping feet echoed in the hallway.

"Try it if you want to," he said reluctantly. "I guarantee you'll be back at the end of the year begging for forty healthy kids."

I filed my transfer request. Again. And the new semester found me happily independent with a briefcase of my favorite books and a stack of three-by-five cards, each stating the name and affliction of one homebound or hospitalized student. It was my responsibility to bring an assignment to each bedside, five to the working day. I was teaching and yet I was free. And my first group of students were not pitifully afflicted. Each was simply homebound with a case of temporary *cyesis*.

My first student was Elmire Watson. She greeted me at the door, her *cyesis* immediately evident, about the eighth month of it. She waited for me to enter, her hand resting on her stomach, the way women sometimes stand in the late months. She was fifteen and she needed to complete tenth-grade English. Through an open bedroom door I could see two other small children—her sister's baby, she explained, and her own small brother. Her mother had already left for work but the apart-

ment was tidy and warm and a little pot of coffee
intended for me rested on the stove. And Elmira
was prepared, three little sharpened pencils like
sentinels beside her notebook on the scrubbed
kitchen table.

"You want my homework?" she asked me.

I did. Proudly she handed me her paragraph,
written in a large square hand.

> What is important to me. I do want a big weding
> with a white dress and a specal cake. I want the
> bridesmates in pink and a live band. But the baby
> is coming but it dont matter. My mother promised
> me the weding after.

She watched me make the corrections and mark
the appropriate square in the grade book which
was to her something magical. With pleasure she
replaced the paper in her thick notebook of graded
papers. She also explained that she was eager to
have *nouns* because she didn't know *nouns* and
once the baby came she might never get the chance
to learn *nouns*. She delighted me. And her *cyesis*
was no impediment to my teaching. I could not
have asked for a more pleasureful hour. Let J.
chew on that.

Unfortunately Velma Smith's house wasn't as
tidy. Old newspapers and trash caught in the tall
grasses of the front yard, and the skeleton of a
Ford station wagon blocked the driveway. It must
have died there and been stripped of all its usable
parts until only the dull shell remained, wedged
into the soil, eroded back to its base metal.

The house was too hot. The stove in the cluttered kitchen burned with the oven door open,
and several mucusy children stood about fingering
the books or climbing up on my lap to see me
write. Parts of breakfast were still on the table.

I am very resilient but I can't stand heat. "Can

we open the window please, Velma? We can't think without air."

She shrugged and opened one of the cracked windows.

"Can you turn off the stove?"

"The kids have colds," she protested.

"And do you think your mother might take care of the children while we have our lessons?"

I had tried holding the youngest on my lap but she dripped onto the grade book. I felt rotten as Velma shoved the protesting children into a bedroom and made a few swipes at clearing the table. I started my lecture on the importance of learning to communicate when I spotted a mouse. My response to mice is entirely involuntary. I lifted my feet to let it pass and I followed its voyage across the cluttered room with considerable alarm. When I returned to Velma her eyes were angry. And I was ashamed of my reaction. I mean you can't blame a girl for a mouse.

"So what!" she said defensively. "We got a cat!"

•

"I didn't mean to be critical," I explained to J. that evening on the phone. "I have a problem with mice."

"I told you it wasn't your vocation. You wanted a more personal encounter and mice are come under the category of personal encounters."

"Mice are too personal."

"Do you know what you're looking for? Have you any idea what personal means? Personal isn't Molly Bloom's soliloquy or Hamlet's monologue. Hamlet talking to himself isn't personal. *Mice* are personal."

I had no intention of debating the point. But it was fortuitous that Mrs. Vanderveld's husband made his sudden decision to retire.

"Would you consider teaching in a maternity home?" begged my supervisor. "Mrs. Vanderveld up and left without notice for Tucson, Arizona. Her ungraded papers are still on her desk. Huntington House desperately needs an English teacher."

I would not admit it to J. but I desperately needed Huntington House.

"You're out of your mind!" said J. "If only one pregnant girl presses in, a whole school of them will stifle you."

"It was the mouse," I protested. "A maternity home would never tolerate mice. And the classes are small. And with all that time on their hands, they'll be delighted to do *Julius Ceasar*."

I dragged J. across town to where Huntington House was located, a poor neighborhood in a forgotten corner of the city, with a certain quietness, a certain rural atmosphere that appealed to my spirit, a solitude that I think I had been searching for all along. Old frame houses with uneven porches, sloping and wind-dried but swept clean and made joyful with containers of flowers.

"I've never seen so many pregnant girls," marveled J. It did seem that way. Pregnant girls strolled the sidewalks in groups of twos or threes. Although there didn't seem many likely places to stroll. A drugstore, a self-service laundry, a tortilleria, a little coffee shop called Joe's Quicke Lunche, a very small supermarket, one dirty pet shop where the owner had jammed his puppies tightly into cages so that they climbed over each other's silken bodies to get to the bars with their damp noses. One little fat girl who seemed too young to be carrying a baby of her own leaned against the dirty glass to watch them.

"If you think this is the answer you're crazy," said J. over coffee in Joe's Quicke Lunche. "Why on earth would you want to teach in a maternity home? You'll miss the male response." J. has a certain egotism. "How are you going to teach 'Prufrock' to nervous, frightened pregnant girls? Just ask yourself, what can you teach pregnant girls that they don't already know?"

It was my intention on that optimistic afternoon to teach them composition and vocabulary and literature analysis. Everything that a smart teacher with a Master's in English can teach to high-school girls. I couldn't know then that I would also learn a lesson, a significant and vital lesson, from a sixteen-year-old girl without any judgment, without any logic, without any husband, with nothing as her text but an unborn baby named Heather.

Love's Labour's Lost

The VW bus was probably parked in the driveway when I arrived but I had not noticed it because as I climbed the steps I was worrying about Calpurnia.

The stone steps of Huntington House make a turn to the right before rising toward the double doors of the entry and I had paused at the turn to consider the problem of Caesar's wife. Calpurnia could bear no children. Caesar had specifically commanded Marc Antony, "Forget not in your speed, Antonius, to touch Calpurnia, for our elders say the barren, touched in this holy chase, shake off their sterile curse." Could I teach *Julius Caesar* without editing the script for students among whom not one was barren, not one was sterile? How could I explain Marc Antony running naked on the Feast of the Lupercal, trying to make Caesar's wife pregnant by hitting her with a goatskin whip? Could I discuss the phallic symbolism of the whip without getting too personal? Anyhow could I assume that pregnant girls knew more about sex than non-pregnant girls? Non-pregnant girls knew enough not to get pregnant.

If pregnant unwed girls read *Ethan Frome*, would there be a painful stirring of the ashes of old fires? Poor Ethan, longing with mute passion for his sweet young cousin and tied to his tooth-less old wife. Should I assume that pregnant girls suffered from unrequited love? Maybe they suf-fered from requited love. Maybe from love by force. Maybe from carelessness, with no love at all. Could I teach "How do I love thee? Let me count the ways"? What if someone cried? Bad enough *I* cried.

And so I didn't notice the girl who came up behind me until I heard a car door slam. A VW camping bus was backing out of the driveway and she had paused beside me on the turn to watch it go.

"God," she said in panic, "I blew it. I really blew it."

She stood for a moment, hovering before she continued, little wing bones of her shoulders clear against the thin tight shirt she wore, lithe girl with the tan of the outdoors still on her and a small obvious bulge where she had loosened the top buttons of her jeans. Which presented me with a further question. What does one say to a pregnant girl who carries a knapsack and wears her hair tied with an Indian band? She had spoken first. And she was in distress, her eyes fixed on the cor-ner where the bus had disappeared. I could almost follow her fantasy the way I could follow her eyes —the bus would swing around, screech to a stop, she would fly down those steps again. But no car returned, and I could see her panic resolve itself into a bleak acceptance. She looked to me and shrugged her shoulders. And so I felt obliged to offer some words of solace. I searched for some-thing appropriate, and literary.

"Don't worry," I said, in what I hoped was a warm tone. "The sun also *rises*."

She glanced quizzically in my direction but she did not reply.

"The sun *sets*," I explained, "but the sun also *rises*."

"You're kidding," she said, and together we turned and climbed toward the entry. She dragged the knapsack of streaked canvas behind her, scraping the steps with it. She hesitated long enough to look over at me, to whip back the yellow hair with a horsetail flick. "Is that a cryptic saying or something?"

"It's the title of a novel by Ernest Hemingway."

"I never heard of it."

"Read it. The book gives meaning to the title."

I pulled the door open for her. She stood on the threshold, perplexed. "You actually mean that you want me to read a whole book so that I can figure out the title and get an answer to the little thing I just happened to say to you?"

"I suppose that's what I implied."

"Stupid," she said. "Really stupid."

She was absolutely right.

The door closed behind us. She dropped her knapsack in the entry, bent over it rummaging for something while I surveyed the bleak room. To the left a little alcove for visitors, a plastic sofa scarred by cigarette burns, some bland pastoral prints hanging crooked on enameled walls. Depressing. A door to the hallway through which I could see pregnant girls passing, none interested enough to give us more than a cursory glance. And to the right a glass door marked OFFICE. Three doors like three wishes or three feathers. Trinities have always fascinated me. I always get good paragraphs on trinities. Three blind mice, three little pigs. All that.

"Do you want a feel of my rock?" asked the

Indian band. She held out what she had been searching for—a black rock, a beautiful oval stone which rested in the palm of her hand.

"Is that obsidian?" I asked her.

"Jesus, you're not supposed to label it. You're just supposed to feel it." She withdrew the stone, stood rubbing it against her cheek.

"Why not?" I asked her. "It seems to me that if you understand the history and the structure of the rock, you can enjoy it all the more."

Teaching is an art. Not confined to the classroom.

"Understand a *rock*?" She negated me with a toss of her head. "God!" She kicked off her sandals. Her bare feet were dusty. And familiar.

"Is that Sara?" called a welcoming voice. A tight brisk woman with a clipboard full of notes approached, hand outstretched to the girl from the VW bus. "It's about time. We expected you yesterday."

Sara shook the hand listlessly. "I wasn't in any rush."

"Cheer up," said the clipboard woman. "Huntington isn't so bad. You'll get along all right."

"Have I got any choice?" She kicked her knapsack into a sort of seat and sat on it, bony knees in the air and her head drooping between her shoulders.

The welcoming committee appraised her critically. "Sure you have choices. We always have choices."

"Thanks for the keen advice," she said. "I think I'm going to throw up."

The clipboard woman turned her appraising eyes on me. "Doris is waiting for you in the office. Vanderveld left us in a mess. I hope you don't have a husband with asthma." And then as an afterthought, "I hope you know what you're doing." And then as a mollification, "I'm Rodriguiz. Office open any morning. Coffee's on in the kitchen. If you need it."

I happen to be a tea drinker. But I nodded my thanks and turned toward the office. I glanced about first, I remember, looking for an omen that would bode me well. I am not superstitious. Quite the contrary. But portents have a literary tradition and I searched for a symbol. A certain book on a table or a figure in a picture or a flower. I saw Currier and Ives prints, pots of ivy and cactus, a social worker making notes on a clipboard, and a weary teen-ager, sick to her stomach, empty with the loss of a VW bus, cleaning the dirt-filled nails of her toes. So I looked to my friend T. S. Eliot who advised me to "prepare a face to meet the faces that you meet." I prepared a smiling face and headed toward the office to find a head teacher named Doris.

She meets Doris and gets the teaching job in this school for pregnant teenagers. What follows is "a hilarious and touching recollection. A message all too often forgotten: there are no problem kids, just kids with problems."

—Chicago Sun Times

Be sure to read the complete Bantam Book, available now wherever paperbacks are sold.

WHEN YOU THINK ZINDEL, THINK BANTAM!

If you like novels whose characters are teenagers caught in the tangle of life and love—PAUL ZINDEL is right on your wavelength. All of Zindel's Young Adult novels are now available exclusively from Bantam.

☐	12501	**PARDON ME, YOU'RE STEPPING ON MY EYEBALL!**	$1.95
☐	12741	**MY DARLING, MY HAMBURGER**	$1.95
☐	11829	**CONFESSIONS OF A TEENAGE BABOON**	$1.95
☐	12579	**THE PIGMAN**	$1.95
☐	12774	**I NEVER LOVED YOUR MIND**	$1.95
☐	12548	**THE EFFECT OF GAMMA RAYS ON MAN-IN-THE-MOON MARIGOLDS**	$1.95

TEENAGERS FACE LIFE AND LOVE

Choose books filled with fun and adventure, discovery and disenchantment, failure and conquest, triumph and tragedy, life and love.

☐	13359	**THE LATE GREAT ME** Sandra Scoppettone	$1.95
☐	10946	**HOME BEFORE DARK** Sue Ellen Bridgers	$1.50
☐	11961	**THE GOLDEN SHORES OF HEAVEN** Katie Letcher Lyle	$1.50
☐	12501	**PARDON ME, YOU'RE STEPPING ON MY EYEBALL!** Paul Zindel	$1.95
☐	11091	**A HOUSE FOR JONNIE O.** Blossom Elfman	$1.95
☐	12025	**ONE FAT SUMMER** Robert Lipsyte	$1.75
☐	13184	**I KNOW WHY THE CAGED BIRD SINGS** Maya Angelou	$2.25
☐	13013	**ROLL OF THUNDER, HEAR MY CRY** Mildred Taylor	$1.95
☐	12741	**MY DARLING, MY HAMBURGER** Paul Zindel	$1.95
☐	12420	**THE BELL JAR** Sylvia Plath	$2.50
☐	12338	**WHERE THE RED FERN GROWS** Wilson Rawls	$1.75
☐	11829	**CONFESSIONS OF A TEENAGE BABOON** Paul Zindel	$1.95
☐	11632	**MARY WHITE** Caryl Ledner	$1.95
☐	13352	**SOMETHING FOR JOEY** Richard E. Peck	$1.95
☐	13440	**SUMMER OF MY GERMAN SOLDIER** Bette Greene	$1.95
☐	11839	**WINNING** Robin Brancato	$1.75
☐	13004	**IT'S NOT THE END OF THE WORLD** Judy Blume	$1.75